SCALLOPS AND SORCERERS

THE VAMPIRE KNITTING CLUB: CORNWALL

BOOK TWO

NANCY WARREN

Ambleside Publishing

INTRODUCTION

Jennifer Cunningham is determined to make a success of The Scallop Shell, the knitting shop she's managing in Tregrebi, a pretty fishing village in Cornwall. As a way to increase sales, she decides to hold a knitting and crochet retreat at Shadowbrook Manor, the former Bed and Breakfast Inn where she lives. She and her best friend and fellow witch Lucy Swift Crosyer will co-host the retreat.

However, Jennifer shares the property with a group of vampires who live below ground in an old tin mine and they are less than pleased at the idea of daywalkers coming to Shadowbrook Manor and wandering around at all hours. They try to talk her out of the retreat but, with the help of the gorgeous former pirate Gryffin Penrose, she convinces the vampires the week-long retreat will be trouble free.

She could not have been more wrong.

When one of the retreat guests is murdered, Jennifer becomes uncomfortably aware that she's likely sharing her home with the killer. Can she figure out whodunnit before her first knitting retreat becomes her last?

Join Jennifer and her colorful undead friends in this paranormal cozy mystery. There's no blood, gore, sex or swearing, just good clean murderous fun.

Scallops and Sorcerers is book 2 in the *Vampire Knitting Club: Cornwall* series but the book can be read as a standalone. Join the Vampire Knitting Club today!

Get the origin story of Rafe, the gorgeous, sexy vampire in *The Vampire Knitting Club* series, for free when you join Nancy's no-spam newsletter at NancyWarrenAuthor.com.

Come join Nancy in her private Facebook group where we talk about books, knitting, pets and life. www.facebook.com/groups/NancyWarrenKnitwits

SCALLOPS AND SORCERERS

CHAPTER 1

"*A* knitting retreat? Here?" After that first shocked cry from Gwendolyn Poulsen, who had been a school headmistress after the war who was now a vampire, there was thunderous silence. I'd announced my intention to host a weeklong retreat here in Cornwall, thinking they'd be thrilled to see me trying something innovative. Oh, how wrong I was. Gwendolyn had an air of authority and a very educated way of speaking that made other vampires listen when she spoke.

Unfortunately for me, in this case. Still, I tried to get her, and the rest of the vampire knitting club, on board with my idea. I hadn't lived here long and was still trying to get comfortable knitting with the undead.

"That's right." I kept my tone enthusiastic. As a fledgling business manager trying to make a success of The Scallop Shell knitting shop, I'd been really excited at the prospect of hosting a knitting and crochet retreat. I wanted to have it here in Shadowbrook Manor, where I lived and which had formerly been a bed and breakfast. I mean, put together a knitting shop, a big manor house with a lot of bedrooms and an ocean view—oh yeah, and Cornwall—and a knitting and crochet retreat sounded like it was meant to be.

At least, it did to me. Also to my best friend, Lucy Swift Crosyer, who would travel down from Oxford to co-host the event.

Not so much to a crowd of horrified vampires, some of whom had even stopped knitting to stare at me. "You can't possibly have day walkers here on the property wandering around at all hours," Robin Trebilcock announced. "It's out of the question." Robin had been the gamekeeper here about two hundred years ago and treated anyone who came on the property with about the same welcome he'd have given poachers back in the day.

There was general agreement from the other vampires, who went back to their work. Some were knitting, a few mending nets. We'd stretched the definition of knitting club, as some of the local vampires still put out to sea just like in the old days when they'd been fishermen or pirates or, in some cases, both. Only now they did their sailing late at night.

I hadn't been part of their knitting club for that long, and we were still getting to know each other. I was pretty sure the local vampires thought one lone thirty-year-old American woman would be easy to control. I needed to prove to them that I was not a pushover. Still, I wanted to get along with them, for more reasons than the obvious one that I was never certain they weren't eyeing me up as a potential snack. However, they were well-fed, and none of them bothered to hunt for food anymore. Besides, Rafe Crosyer, who owned the manor house, would not let my unfortunate demise go unpunished, and they all knew it.

Being a witch, I did have some skills and protection spells, but I'd rather not test my strength against a nest of vampires who shared the property. We coexisted pretty well for the most part, me above ground in Rafe and Lucy's gorgeous house and they in their luxurious accommodations below ground in an abandoned tin mine.

"You used to get along okay when this house was run as a bed and breakfast," I reminded them.

"And a very good thing it was when that shut down. Now, Jennifer, you don't want a load of outsiders coming snooping around. You know you don't. You've secrets of your own, haven't you?" Gwendolyn looked at me as though waiting for my answer to a complex math question.

I definitely did, but then, who doesn't have secrets?

I let them talk and tried to concentrate on the sweater I was knitting. I had designed the pattern myself and was thinking of making it an exclusive project for the retreat. I let the annoyed mutterings continue, and then, finally, Agnes Bartlett spoke up. Agnes was Lucy's grandmother and one of the nicest vampires I knew. She hadn't been a vampire for very long, and maybe that was what made her more conscious of my very human needs. Besides, she'd owned the knitting shop in Oxford before Lucy inherited it, and now she was helping me with The Scallop Shell, the pretty little shop I ran on Tregrebi's high street.

"It will only be for a week," she said soothingly. "And you know, if The Scallop Shell isn't successful, who's to say my grandson-in-law won't let Shadowbrook Manor out to a family or another couple who want to run it as a bed and breakfast? A knitting and crochet retreat will help keep The Scallop Shell successful and Jennifer, who is so easy to get along with, here in Tregrebi. It is really in all our best interests. We wouldn't want to lose you, dear."

That got them thinking. I knew that now Rafe had married Lucy, he wanted to keep this place available anytime they felt like popping down to Cornwall, but I doubted the local vampires knew that. Opening a knitting shop here had been a way to get Agnes out of Oxford, where she kept forgetting she was dead and wandering out into Oxford, where she could bump into someone who'd attended her funeral.

Giving her a new home and another shop to think about here in Cornwall kept her out of trouble, but I knew she missed Oxford and Lucy. Keeping her very involved in the Cornwall shop gave her something to do, and besides, we both felt a bit competitive. We'd love to see The Scallop Shell do as well or even better than Cardinal Woolsey's in Oxford. That was one reason why Agnes was an enthusiastic supporter of the retreat. The other, of course, was it meant Lucy would spend the week here with us and probably she'd come down for some planning sessions beforehand so Agnes would get to see her beloved granddaughter.

"Yeah. You're all right," Dougan Hayes said. I was delighted to have support from someone other than Lucy's grandmother. Dougan was an undead Australian surfer who now did his surfing at night.

Then Agnes's best friend, Sylvia Strand, joined the discussion. Sylvia had been a stage and screen star in the 1920s and still did everything with drama. "I for one am very pleased to see Jennifer making a success of The Scallop Shell. It's so convenient having the shop so close when we run out of wool or other supplies."

And they gave the term late-night shopping a whole new meaning.

"But we have our knitting club here. Where are we supposed to go?" Robin Trebilcock asked.

The grumbling and complaints continued even as, between the three of us, we tried to convince the vampires that a weeklong knitting and crochet retreat would be quiet, harmless fun.

We could not have been more wrong.

CHAPTER 2

The nice thing about walking on the coastal path of Cornwall midmorning on a bright, sunny day was that I was in no danger of bumping into anyone from the vampire knitting club. Right now they were collectively the last creatures I wanted to see. I'd been so excited about the idea of our knitting retreat. It was going to be fantastic, a chance to really put The Scallop Shell on the map, since if we did one successful knitting retreat, we would obviously do many more. It was also a way to differentiate my shop—well, what I liked to call my shop—from Lucy's.

But the arguments and negative comments from the local vampires at last night's meeting had really dimmed my enthusiasm. All the vampires had to do was stay out of sight for a week. Was that so much to ask? Couldn't they have their knitting circle down in the tin mine? Or they were always welcome to use the shop late at night when nobody was in there. It wasn't like they hadn't been there before.

I hadn't realized how much they were creatures of habit, so accustomed to sitting around late at night in Rafe's manor house that they didn't want to give up the comfortable space. Even though in the end, obviously, they were going to have to put up with the retreat, I didn't want them to be angry. I was still trying to make my way here and get along. And, frankly, since the full-time population of this small coastal town wasn't that large, I kind of needed the company of the vampires. Call me a creature pleaser, but I didn't want to be at outs with my nearest neighbors, undead or not.

They hadn't been my best friends when they'd ended the meeting last night. In spite of Agnes's arguments and even Sylvia adding her voice of support, it was pretty clear that they considered Sylvia and Agnes as outsiders, only slightly less outsiders than I was, since they were at least also undead. I was definitely the odd person out.

We'd ended the meeting on the coldest of terms.

So what was I going to do? I felt like I wanted to make it up to them somehow, but giving up on the retreat was not an option. I could be stubborn when I needed to be, and right now I was feeling as stubborn as I ever got. How could they not at least try to see things from my point of view? I'd come all the way over from Boston, and I was trying to make a new life here. My best friend in the world still lived hours away in Oxford, and let's face it, now that she was married, it wasn't the same. One of the reasons I was so excited about the retreat was that I would get to spend a week with my best friend, Lucy.

I'd arrived originally for Lucy's wedding and then stayed on with the offer of a job here. Lucy and I both gave it a three-month trial. And the three months turned into six and then nine, and I was pretty sure I was going to make it to a year. If I didn't have a load of undead Debbie Downers complaining about all my ideas for the shop.

Lucy and I had taken a marketing course for independent retailers in Oxford, and in looking for ways to add value to the stores, we'd come up with the idea of a retreat. Okay, it wasn't a particularly original idea, but we were excited at the prospect.

We'd also started to experiment with a few online ads for our two shops. The vampires hadn't liked that either. The fewer people who knew about this area of the world, the better, as far as they were concerned. I didn't want the place overrun with tour buses or anything, but come on, a select group of people who loved to knit and crochet seemed like a fabulous opportunity for our fledgling store.

Every time I'd tried to spin the retreat in a positive way, they stomped all over my enthusiasm with their negative attitudes and complaints. Gryffyn Penrose, who was the unofficial leader of the group, had been away, which hadn't helped. I felt he was more open-minded than some of the other vampires.

I was stomping along, hardly even noticing the blue expanse of the ocean, the jagged rocky cutouts that made up the shoreline, or the haunting sound of the seabirds. Normally I drank in the views and filled my nostrils and lungs with the beautiful sea-tinged air, but today I strode along fuming, going so fast I was out of breath.

A voice said, "You're in quite a hurry there." I'd been looking down at the ground scowling, and I glanced up to see Andrew Jackson coming toward me. Andrew was, if not precisely a new friend, someone I had come to know quite recently. He ran the Bide-a-Spell Bookstore and was a fellow witch. As he came closer, he said, "You look to be in a right strop."

I wasn't completely conversant yet with British slang, but I suspected he was telling me I was in a bad mood. I didn't think you had to have magic powers to be able to see that. It occurred to me that he might be a good ally in my efforts to create this knitting retreat.

I said, "I'm pretty grumpy, if that's what you mean, and I could use some advice. How long are you planning to walk for?"

"As long as you like, if you care to accompany me."

This was exactly what I wanted to hear. We both politely turned in the other's direction and then, since I really wanted to head away from the manor house rather than towards it, I let him bend his direction to mine. Andrew had an open, pleasant face and guileless blue eyes, but underneath the short-sleeved shirt he was wearing, I knew he had a tattoo of Huginn and Muninn, two ravens who were his familiars, and also hidden beneath the buttons of his shirt, a Pentacle, his witch's medallion.

After we walked together for a few steps, he said, "Do you prefer to sulk in silence, or do you want to talk about it?"

I didn't think I was sulking, exactly. I was just perturbed. I said, "Andrew, I'm having a problem, and I think you could help me."

He chuckled. "I always enjoy how direct you Americans are. Very well, I'm all ears, and you know I'll help you if I can. We shopkeepers need to stick together in a small town like this."

There was an unspoken message underneath that we witches also needed to stick together, not only in small towns but in all towns. Despite all the crystal shops and pagan lore and people who rushed to Stonehenge on the solstices, it could still be a pretty lonely life when you were a genuine witch with genuine powers. Not that I didn't believe most people could develop more sensitivity to the supernatural side of life if they let it in, but in my experience, being a witch was either a gift or a curse, however you looked at it, more than something you could learn like, say, playing the cello.

Andrew might know that I was a witch, but he didn't know I lived with vampires, and I was bound by my own sense of honor as well as a promise I had made never to reveal the existence of the vampires. So I said, "I want to run a knitting and crochet retreat right here in Tregrebi."

He waited for more, but that was all I said. He nodded enthusiastically. "I think that's a wonderful idea." He immediately listed all the advantages that of course were obvious. "You've got that lovely manor house with more bedrooms than I can recall. It operated not so long ago as a bed and breakfast, so I'm sure it would be the work of a moment to get it going again." I was nodding away. "And there are knitters and other crafters who would love an excuse to spend a week in a beautiful coastal town in Cornwall. So, I have to ask myself, what are you so upset about?"

Since I couldn't tell him the exact truth, I voiced my second biggest fear. "But what if they don't come? What if I set all this up and I just make a fool of myself?"

Honestly, while I was more annoyed about the lack of support from my undead friends, I really was worried that I would put in a lot of effort and set up expectations that I couldn't meet. That would be humiliating. The retreat had been my idea. While Lucy had been immediately supportive, it was still her shop and basically her money that would get the whole thing going. If the retreat was a failure, then I'd feel like a failure.

Andrew seemed to understand my dilemma without me having to explain it. "Well, when I try something new and I'm afraid of failure, I do everything I can to make that failure impossible."

That was sensible advice. I turned toward him, slowing my steps. "Go on."

"I'm not a knitter, but if I were going to organize, let's say, a small literary festival here, I would think about where I was going to get authors to come and speak. And frankly, that would be the easiest thing of all."

"We don't have that problem. My friend Lucy will teach beginners, and I'll teach intermediate. I'm worried that we won't get enough knitters to make it worthwhile."

"Yes, that would be the thing that would worry me the most, too." He looked at me. "How many do you need?"

Okay, I'd sat up late at night on the computer playing with different variables. I knew the numbers by heart now, so I just went through what I'd come up with last night. "There are eight bedrooms. A few are twin rooms, so two could share, which would be cheaper, and some people will want to pay more and have their own rooms. I calculated that we could host twelve people comfortably. Lucy and I can stay in the quarters where the couple who ran the bed and breakfast used to live."

"That's excellent. And what if you don't get twelve?"

I was glad he'd asked that, because I was pretty sure we wouldn't get twelve on our first time out, and twelve seemed like too many anyway. "Obviously, I am trying to run a business here. I want a small profit, but we'll do that with eight participants."

"I'm glad to hear it. The way you were talking, I was worried that you were planning to run this like a charity operation, and let me tell you, my dear, that is the road to a shuttered and boarded retail establishment. I don't care how many advantages you have, you must run your knitting and crochet retreat like the business it is."

I told him the price I was thinking of. Not that he was the best person to ask; as he'd said himself, he didn't knit, and he ran a bookshop, but since he was a native of the area, I wanted to see if he balked. I had based the price on similar types of retreats that I'd seen advertised online, and I knew that even at eight people, we would make a small profit. At twelve, it would be a rousing success. And anywhere between those two numbers, I'd be more than happy. If we only had six sign up, I had to wonder if it was worth running the retreat at all. And, of course, even though our rent was basically free and Mr. and Mrs. Biddle were on-site, they would probably need extra help.

Andrew asked for a few more details, so I was able to tell him we planned to provide breakfast and afternoon tea every day and the guests would be on their own for dinner.

"That price sounds more than fair to me," he said when I'd outlined the rough program.

He suggested that we run the ad purely in our newsletters first with some kind of early bird discount. I thought that was an excellent idea and one I hadn't thought of. His argument was that it might fill up right away, and if it didn't, then we would know that we had more work to put into the advertising or we'd gotten something wrong. He also said he would happily put a poster up in his window and would make sure he had a display of knitting and crochet books as well as lots of books of local interest. He thought for a moment. "I might even offer a discount to your knitters and crocheters."

I was delighted. Not only because he had given me such sensible advice, but clearly from the fact that he was already thinking about stocking his bookshop and giving discounts, he believed in the retreat. There's nothing like somebody adding their own ideas to make you realize that they believe in what you're doing. If he'd just been wanting to be nice, he would have murmured appreciation and said yes at the appropriate places, but he sounded genuinely engaged with the idea and quite enthusiastic.

We chatted a bit more about the logistics, and then he said, "In fact, you know, Jennifer, if your retreat is successful, and I thoroughly believe it will be, perhaps I will think about a little literary festival."

I twinkled at him. "And if you do, I will offer your festival customers a discount in my knitting shop."

He chuckled. "I see that we understand one another."

Even though I couldn't tell him about my real worry, the fact that he was so supportive made me incredibly happy and calmed me down enormously. I was going to have my knitting retreat, whatever the moaning vampires argued, and I was going to make it work.

I felt much better when I got back to Shadowbrook Manor. Talking to Andrew had calmed me down and made me see reason. I walked in the front door in a much better mood than when I'd left it. I headed toward the stairs to go up to my room when something made me glance into the living room, or the lounge as they called it here, and I nearly jumped out of my skin when I noticed a man standing at the window with his back to me, staring out to sea. Now since the bed and breakfast managers had moved out, I had been living here alone but for the caretakers, who had their own cottage on the property. Mrs. Biddle was often in the kitchen but never in the lounge unless she was cleaning or serving food there. Mr. Biddle stayed outside unless he was required to fix something in the house, but that was rare. So to find a strange man standing staring out to sea was enough to have me ready with my magic, but as I readied my hands, he turned around, and I recognized the vampire pirate Gryffyn Penrose. Also, I now noticed my familiar, Busby, was rubbing up against the pirate's legs, demanding attention.

"What are you doing here?" I asked him, more sharply than I would have, if he'd knocked on the front door like a normal person.

He raised his eyebrows at that. "I'm sorry. I didn't mean to startle you." He picked up the cat, and she curled against him as though his chest was her happy place, which I thought it was. She began to purr so loudly I had to raise my voice.

"The thing is, in my world, when people come visiting, they normally give some indication of their intention. They don't just appear in the middle of a person's living space."

"Are you otherwise engaged?" He glanced around as though thinking I might have invisible visitors.

"No. That's not the point. It's polite to ring the doorbell or knock on the door. Maybe send me a text message and tell me you're coming."

"You see, I tend to avoid front doors, especially on a day like today."

I immediately felt guilty. It was a bright, sunny day. What

had I been thinking? Of course he couldn't wander down the high street, stop to smell the roses, and then stand in the full sun knocking on my door, waiting for me to answer it—or not, if I wasn't home.

"Never mind," I said. "Now that you're here, what's up?"

I had a sneaking suspicion I knew what was up, but I wanted to hear him tell me in his own way. He rocked back on his heels. "I understand there was a bit of bother last night at the knitting club," he said at last.

"It was more than a spot of bother. It was an argument, and to be honest, I was quite shocked. I believe that all the vampires living in the tin mine are essentially Rafe Crosyer's guests. So when his wife and her best friend want to put on a knitting retreat, and all we ask is that they stay out of sight for a week, it doesn't seem like that should lead to such a big argument."

He nodded, his deep green eyes staring into mine so I felt I had his full attention. Well, except for the rhythmic way he was stroking the cat. "I understand your point. But I wish you could see things through our eyes. We've been hunted and persecuted for so long, and finally we have these little pockets of peace." He held up a hand before I could speak. "I know what you're going to say. Yes, we had a bed and breakfast running here for some twenty years. But before that, there was no one. Twenty years to us is the blink of an eye. So to have you contemplating bringing day walkers in again, when we aren't even quite used to you yet, is causing a bit of turmoil."

I waved him to a seat, where Busby curled up in his lap, and sat down myself. "Honestly, if you'd been there last night, I feel like we could have sorted it out easily. As it was, there were only Agnes Bartlett and Sylvia Strand speaking up in defense of our project, but I get the feeling that the Cornwall vampires don't trust Agnes and Sylvia yet, either."

"It's not a case of not trusting; it's just that they haven't been here very long. We aren't used to them yet, either."

I could perfectly understand that, but I still thought my point was valid. "Dougan Hayes seemed like he was on our side, but I don't think his opinion holds as much weight as some of the others."

"You're right, there."

I said, "Couldn't they all go stay with you for a week? You've got that big, beautiful manor house."

"But they all have their own quarters in the tin mine, and that's where they like to be. If we tried to move them out, that would just make more trouble."

"You're not asking me to cancel the knitting and crochet retreat, are you?"

He paused, and I felt like he'd hoped I would voluntarily cancel the project. "No. I suppose not. I respect your abilities as a businesswoman and your desire to make a profit. It's just come as a bit of a shock, that's all." And then his eyes lit with a rueful twinkle. "Besides, everyone looks forward to the knitting club. We've become accustomed to having it here. That will have to move."

I heartily agreed. The last thing I wanted was some poor knitting retreat participant to need a glass of water in the middle of the night and wander into a bunch of undead knitters. The very idea made me shudder.

"What about your place?" I said again. "You've definitely got plenty of room to host a knitting meeting."

He nodded. "We could, but if we must move it, mightn't

we have it in the upstairs of the knitting shop? There's plenty of room up there and also easy access if anybody runs out of wool or other supplies."

I'd known when Lucy and Rafe bought the shop that the upstairs apartment could easily host a knitting circle, and I thought the same thing. I was still curious why he didn't want to have it at his house, but I didn't want to get into any more arguments with vampires. I'd had enough of that.

"We'll have to do something about blocking out the light from the windows so no locals wonder what's going on," I reminded him.

"That should be easy. We'll have proper blackout blinds fitted. It will be like being back in World War II."

I loved how they could so easily reference points in history that they remembered the way I remembered wearing braces in grade school.

"Exactly," I agreed.

He nodded and rose, to Busby's immediate heartbreak. She rolled over and stuck all four feet in the air until he laughed and patted her belly. "That's all right then. If you're willing to move the knitting club to the shop, I'll talk to my friends. Make sure there's no trouble."

"I would really appreciate that." Because, in the same way that they were getting used to Sylvia and Agnes, I was getting used to coexisting with the vampires. The thoughts that sprang into my head of the kind of trouble they could cause made my stomach lurch.

CHAPTER 3

The Biddles, the couple Rafe had hired to remain at Shadowbrook Manor even after the bed and breakfast closed, were supposed to look after the place and, even though I felt very uncomfortable, to look after me. Mr. Biddle was usually outside in the grounds or doing the odd jobs, and Mrs. Biddle took care of the kitchen and the food and the housekeeping in the main house. We'd had a few difficult moments, but I'd finally convinced her that I did not want my room cleaned and I liked to have access to the kitchen to do my own cooking or at least make my own coffee. However, you can't live with people and not find compromise, so I tended to let her cook breakfast for me, and if I came home after a busy day at the shop and found dinner was ready, was I going to refuse it?

Needless to say, it was important to get her cooperation for the retreat. I thought she'd be thrilled to have more people to cook for than me, but instead of being pleased, she was horribly negative. Much like the vampires. Maybe I presented it to her badly, assuming she'd be delighted, and then she immediately declared the opposite.

She said she was too old to run around after a dozen women, picking up bits of stray wool and thread off the carpet. And she couldn't possibly manage an afternoon tea every day. Now, I figured one of my selling points on this retreat was to have a proper Cornish afternoon tea.

We might have remained at a standstill, but luckily Lucy and Rafe came down for a few days to have a planning session. When I told Lucy that Mrs. Biddle had balked at providing afternoon tea, Lucy was much more understanding than I'd been. "She's probably feeling overwhelmed. Why don't we ask Agatha Trevellen at The Cornish Teapot if they would like to bring an afternoon tea every day?"

As it turned out, this suggestion was a stroke of brilliance. Neither of us knew that there was an intense rivalry between Mrs. Biddle and Mrs. Trevellen until the moment Lucy offered the idea to Mrs. Biddle. It turned out they both prided themselves on making the best scones in Tregrebi. Just the thought of having her archrival cooking in her kitchen was more than Mrs. Biddle could bear. So, having said she wouldn't make afternoon tea, she then turned around and said that anybody else would be in her kitchen making scones and messing up her things over her dead body.

Then Rafe mentioned that he appreciated how much extra work the retreat would entail and there would be a nice bonus for his two faithful retainers for putting up with the upheaval and helping during Lucy and Jennifer's first knitting and crochet retreat, and that sealed the deal. She might get irritable and difficult with two young women from America, but Rafe was her hero.

When we were alone in the lounge, Lucy threw her arms around him and said, "How do you do it? We could barely get Mrs. Biddle to stop moaning about all the extra work, and then you come along and she can't do enough."

He accepted her hug and her praise and smiled down at her in a way that made me realize why she had fallen for him. He really was devilishly attractive. "Don't forget, my dear, I've been around this Earth a long time and learned to deal with much more difficult people than the Biddles. It's a question of making them want the thing you wish them to do. In this case, Mrs. Biddle loves to feel important, and with the teas and the breakfasts, she'll be very much needed and appreciated."

I was tempted to ask him to use the same persuasive methods on the local vampires, but something stopped me. Some sense that his interference might be resented. The Cornish vampires were different from the Oxford ones. And, while Rafe owned this property, it was pretty clear that Gryffyn was their leader and the one they'd listen to. I knew Gryff would do his best to bring the local underground knitting group to at least tolerate the upheaval and decided to leave it at that.

We had a great time planning the retreat, which we set for the end of May, when the weather would hopefully be pleasant and the tourists not too plentiful.

And then Rafe suggested that Mrs. Biddle might like to make me and Lucy an afternoon tea so we'd be better able to advertise its delights. I knew darn well that if we'd asked, she'd have gone all sniffy, but with Rafe, she'd practically danced back to the kitchen to get out the flour and start working on the scones. I thought Rafe could teach a course in human resources management, the way he handled the Biddles.

We didn't dare go near the kitchen the rest of the morning, which was just as well because she'd already fed us well on what she called the full Cornish breakfast, and it was indeed full. In addition to eggs, bacon, sausage, beans, and fried tomato were mushrooms, potato cakes, and something she called hog's pudding. Naturally, she also served toast with butter and her homemade marmalade.

After stuffing ourselves, Lucy and I sat comfortably in the lounge room, occasionally looking out to sea to admire the view and planning out our weeklong retreat, and then taking breaks to gossip and catch up.

"How are you doing here, Jen?" she asked me in one of those catch-up breaks, not in the kind of "how's it going" sort of way but as someone who really wanted to know the truth. And because she was my best friend and had asked me to open and manage The Scallop Shell for her, I was honest.

"It's lonely sometimes, and frankly our late-night knitting club can be a little annoying, gossiping about creatures I've never met and forgetting I'm an outsider. But they're good company, too."

She looked a bit concerned. "Are you making friends? I remember when I first moved to Oxford how challenging I found it until I made my home here. Everyone hears your accent and figures you're on a two-week holiday and heading off on a plane soon. They don't want to invest in a relationship that could be temporary."

I thought about that. Was that true? "I don't know. I think

because I'm managing the store, I'm obviously part of the community, for now at least. There's Agatha Trevellen and her daughter Claire, who run The Cornish Teapot, and the other shopkeepers are nice. There's another witch in town you know, Andrew Jackson—"

Her eyebrows rose. "He's not the seventh president of the United States come to Cornwall as a vampire, is he?"

I chuckled at the very idea. "No. He's not a vampire at all. He's just a witch. He runs the bookshop here in town. Bide-a-Spell books. When we see each other, we always have a good chat, and he gave me some good advice about the retreat."

"Really?" Lucy looked quite impressed. "Is there a local coven nearby?"

I shrugged. "Probably, but I haven't asked."

When Lucy asked, as I'd known she would, if there were any interesting men in the area, I shook my head. But after my last romantic entanglement, I was in no hurry. No hurry at all.

After a couple of hours, we had a solid plan, and then I drafted an article for Lucy's shop newsletter and mine, Lucy's newsletter database being much larger than mine, obviously. We'd decided to begin by only advertising to our subscribers and see if we got enough takers. We also took Andrew's advice and offered an early bird discount. We both agreed that for this first one, we'd cap registration at ten people. If we didn't get eight people signed up, we might have to advertise a bit farther afield. I also decided to put a notice in the window of The Scallop Shell, because locals might want to come or know someone who did, and besides, if I simply put a sign on the window, it would save speculation and gossip.

At three o'clock on the dot, Mrs. Biddle walked in with a huge tray laden with mouthwatering-looking treats on a three-tier cake stand. I spied scones, tiny sandwiches, and, on the top tier, little cakes and pastries. A large pot of tea weighed down one end of the tray. Lucy jumped up to help, but Mrs. Biddle waved her away by jerking an authoritative shoulder. She'd obviously done this plenty of times before. She set the tray on the table by the window and took a moment to catch her breath. We settled ourselves on either side of the table.

"This looks amazing," I said. And it did. I'd had afternoon tea a couple of times in my life but nothing that ever looked like this. I caught her glancing around and suspected she was hoping that Rafe might be in the room to see her creation.

Lucy obviously caught on as well because she said, "Perhaps you could bring a third cup, Mrs. Biddle. I think Rafe will be joining us."

Nothing could have given the housekeeper more pleasure. Then she left and reemerged in less than two minutes with a fresh cup. We'd been smart enough not to touch the tea while she was gone. Sure enough, she gave us a nod and said, "Your tea should be properly steeped by now. Four minutes exactly. You've got milk and sugar. I don't do lemon slices unless particularly asked." Then she glared at both of us, and we shook our heads, not daring to ask for lemon.

We each poured ourselves a cup of tea, and she explained there were both fruit scones and plain. She drilled us with a hard gaze. "And naturally you'll be eating your scones the Cornish way. That is, we put the jam on the scone first, followed by clotted cream. The people of Devon do it the other way round." And it was pretty clear what she thought of the people of Devon.

Both the raspberry and the strawberry jam were home-made, and the finger sandwiches were standard fare but done beautifully. There was smoked salmon with dill, as well as deviled egg, roast beef with just a touch of horseradish, and ham and grainy mustard. For the cakey treats, she'd really outdone herself. There were beautiful, tiny individual lemon drizzle loaves, Cornish saffron cake, a raspberry tart, and again in a practical, disapproving tone she said, "And choco-late cake, of course, which is what the Americans always want."

I thought that was quite unfair. Lucy and I both lived here, and I had never once asked her for chocolate cake. Not that I was going to turn one down. I personally loved choco-late cake, but she didn't have to be mean about it.

Lucy had quickly texted Rafe, and to our great relief, he showed up while Mrs. Biddle was telling us to ring the bell if we needed more hot water or more of anything because she had plenty in the kitchen. As I had suspected, he was lavish in his praise of the afternoon tea, claimed he couldn't wait to tuck in, and thanked her profusely. And then with a twinkle in his eye, he said, "And you don't have to tell me to eat those scones the Cornish way."

She looked delighted, and for a second I caught a glimpse of what she must have been like as a young woman. Then she left, and Rafe sat down. "How's the planning going?" he asked us.

The pair of us shared our ideas for the retreat, including posting a few of the photos we'd snapped of Mrs. Biddle's amazing Cornish afternoon tea, and he listened. Lucy poured him a cup of tea exactly the way she liked it, and as soon as she finished her own tea, she smoothly switched cups with him. The same with the food. They were so practiced at their routine, I barely noticed when she replaced her empty plate with his full one. Naturally, she was only putting half the food on each of their plates, but still, it was an impressive sleight of hand.

I might not like Mrs. Biddle particularly, but she was an amazing cook. After dutifully polishing off the sandwiches, we started on the scones, which were crunchy on the outside and light and fluffy on the inside. Her homemade jam had exactly the right level of sweetness to bring out the fruit's flavor, and the Cornish clotted cream had me wanting to lick the spoon. It was heavy and thicker than whipped cream, and oh, the flavor. And then, even though we were almost too full, we attacked the cake section. Everything was delicious, but I was almost chagrined that I liked the chocolate cake the best. Mrs. Biddle might make it reluctantly, but she made her chocolate cake fabulously.

When we were practically groaning from eating so much food and on our final cup of tea, she came in to clear. When Rafe gave a quick dab at his mouth with a napkin and complimented her again on how delicious it all was, Lucy and I enthusiastically concurred, and more realistically, since we'd actually tasted the food. But Mrs. Biddle, naturally, only had eyes and ears for Rafe.

Then, probably because he was in the room, she looked at Lucy and me. "Would you want your tea exactly like that for your paid guests? Would you want any changes?"

We weren't fools. "Mrs. Biddle," I said, "that was perfect." Lucy agreed.

"I'll serve the same scones every day, but obviously I'll change the sandwiches and the cake so it's a different afternoon tea you'll be having every day."

Lucy got a worried look on her face. "I hate to even ask, but—"

Mrs. Biddle put up her hands. "I know. There's always at least one who's gluten-free or dairy-free or doesn't eat egg or something. I'm well-versed with people's peculiar palates. Don't worry."

That was a relief.

Rafe said, "We know the food will be in excellent hands then, Mrs. Biddle."

She'd already agreed to do both cooked and buffet breakfasts, so both those who just wanted a croissant and a bowl of fruit would be accommodated along with those who liked something more hearty.

After she'd cleared away the tea, Lucy and I read over our newsletters, then we sent them out electronically. It was an exciting moment. Not as exciting as when I'd first opened the shop, but we were trying something new. It was a chance to test both our abilities to run a retreat and put a bit of life back into Shadowbrook Manor.

Still, worry niggled at me. Would anyone sign up? Would all our hope and planning be wasted?

That question was soon answered. Before dinnertime, we had four people signed up, one from my newsletter and three from Lucy's. That early bird discount had been a brilliant idea. We high-fived each other, and Rafe insisted that if we already had four people, we'd be selling out in no time, and then he opened a bottle of champagne for us to celebrate. He was like that. He had a fancy wine cellar here just like he had presumably in all his other homes. I was no connoisseur of champagne, but I suspected this was a good one. The bottle looked old and fancy, and the champagne was pale gold with tiny bubbles that danced on my tongue.

"Who signed up?" Lucy asked as I was on the computer checking the bookings. I read out the names. Two were customers whose names she recognized, Rosalind Wallace and Beatrice Huntington-Cole. We'd asked for people's birthdays (though it was optional), as we sent a card with a shop discount, but Rosalind had also put her year of birth, so we knew that Rosalind Wallace was seventy years old. Beatrice let us know she was born on November tenth.

I was fairly certain the single person who'd so far signed up from my list was a woman from London who'd been down on holiday and loved Cornwall. Sunita Rai was her name, and she loved to crochet. She was forty-five.

Then I said, "Oh, no."

"What is it?" Lucy asked, leaning over my shoulder to peer at the computer screen.

"Oh," she said when she saw the most recent booking. "Anthea Fitzgerald signed up." Her tone was not enthusiastic. Anthea Fitzgerald had been a fellow student at our marketing course in Oxford. She operated a shop in the Lake District, where she sold her own line of soaps and creams. She prided herself, and boasted often, about how everything she made was from local, organic ingredients. She wore a lot of hemp and flax, and I imagined her carbon footprint would be the size of a gnat's. She was also someone I'd have been happy never to see again.

"I remember her saying she'd love to come when we

talked about doing a retreat, but I never dreamed she was serious," I replied.

"Shouldn't she be in the Lake District selling her natural soaps and body creams?" Lucy asked.

I felt uneasy simply seeing her name. I hadn't warmed to Anthea. "Margaret Twigg is convinced she lied about everything being organic and grown locally, as some of her ingredients won't grow in the Lake District where she lives."

"I remember that. Does she even knit?"

"I have no idea. But I don't relish spending an entire week with her."

"No. I always think if a person lies about one thing, what else are they lying about?"

I chuckled. "We tell a few lies ourselves."

Lucy nodded, acknowledging the truth of the hidden parts of our lives. "That's true, but only to protect ourselves and those we care about. Lying about your business products seems more like cheating."

I knew exactly what she meant.

There wasn't much we could do about Anthea coming to our retreat, but it dimmed my pleasure a bit to know she'd be among us, probably trying to sell her wares to our knitters.

Then a wonderful interruption occurred in the shape of Agnes Bartlett, who came in by the French doors. She carried a parasol, which I knew was made of one of those UV-protecting high-tech fabrics.

She and Lucy embraced, and both cried out that they missed each other.

"And how is dear Cardinal Woolsey's?" Agnes asked. She wanted to know all about how the shop was doing and asked after her vampire friends who lived beneath the shop.

I was content to listen.

And then naturally, while Rafe and Lucy were there, we had to host a vampire knitting club.

What the Biddles ever made of these late-night knitting clubs, I had no idea. They'd obviously been turning a blind eye for twenty years and would continue to do so.

CHAPTER 4

*A*t ten, the vampires began to gather in the breakfast room. I could see they'd made an extra effort to arrive on time and look their best, probably because Rafe was present. He was their landlord, after all.

Gryff arrived promptly with his seafaring crew. He tended to dress like a modern man during the day, a somewhat eccentric one, with his long hair and linen shirts. But after dark, he went for the Regency pirate look—leather and buckskin and a sword by his side. When he and Rafe stood together, it was like a meeting of Poldark and Mr. Darcy, albeit cooler and paler.

I knew most of the Cornish vampires who arrived. They greeted me and then sat down to work. Alfred, a vampire who'd come down from Oxford with Sylvia and Agnes and frequently drove Sylvia's Bentley, seemed delighted to see Rafe and Lucy. I got the feeling he missed Oxford.

We all got to work, and then a woman swept in, even more dramatically than Sylvia, if that was possible. She was an extraordinary creature. Tall and buxom, with long auburn hair, she wore a sleeveless long tunic that showed off muscular arms and shoulders I envied immediately. Her gaze swept the room, and she said, "Please, don't get up." Her accent was difficult to place. Somewhere between Swedish, German, and Irish, I thought.

No one jumped to their feet, but Gryff rose leisurely and said, "Ah, Svanhilde. I heard you were in England. Is this a pleasant surprise?" There was an edge to his voice, and I felt a frisson of nervous energy flutter around the room. All eyes turned to the woman, and then Svanhilde laughed. "Indeed it is. Most pleasant." She strode forward and clasped Gryff to her bosom. He pulled away and said, mainly to me and Rafe and Lucy, "This is Svanhilde. My maker."

Now I was even more curious. This was the woman who'd turned Gryffyn Penrose into a vampire? She nodded. "I am Svanhilde. The Viking warrior princess. No doubt you have heard of me?" She glanced toward me and Lucy, but we were clearly mystified. Feeling something was required, I remarked on her interesting name. She nodded and explained. "Svan because I am as beautiful as a swan, and hilde for battle, in which I am fierce."

I could well believe it. I wondered if she got those amazing arms from rowing her own battleship and then jumping on shore for a spot of hand-to-hand combat.

A woman who looked about a foot shorter than Svanhilde came in behind her. She had a cap of straight blond hair and bright blue eyes, and wore tweed trousers and a short jacket. "Georgie," Sylvia cried, getting up to hug the new arrival. With one arm around Georgie, she turned her toward where Rafe and Lucy and I were sitting together. "You must have heard of Georgie Detweiller."

What was it with these formerly famous people? I had no idea who this was, and obviously Lucy didn't either. Rafe rose and went forward to shake the woman's hand. He obviously knew who she was. "I was privileged to watch you play in the Curtis Cup, 1933 or '34, it must have been."

She turned to him with a big smile. "That's right. It was the highlight of my career."

"What brings you to Cornwall?" he asked politely.

"I met Sally in Copenhagen, and we decided to come to England. She wanted to see Gryffyn, I think."

"Sally?" My eyebrows rose.

Georgie glanced at the Viking princess with humor brightening her already bright blue eyes. "By night she's Svanhilde, but during the daytime, we get less attention if I just call her Sally."

I suspected that whatever she was called, Svanhilde/Sally was going to be noticed. Rafe then introduced the two women to me and Lucy. When they got to me, Svanhilde said, "Ah, you are Cornish also?"

"No. I'm from Boston."

"But your name is Cornish."

I glanced around, and there was general nodding. Gryff said, "It's true. Jennifer comes from Guinevere, wife of Arthur."

"And a lovely woman she was," Svanhilde announced, "but not as good with a sword as me."

"How are you with a pair of knitting needles?" Gwendolyn Poulsen asked. I felt that she was calling her class to order. Svanhilde surveyed the room, and since Gryff and Rafe sat together, obviously old friends, and Georgie was already settling beside Sylvia, the Viking princess sat down beside

Robin Trebilcock. He'd never struck me as a chatty fellow, but soon they were talking about the hunting they'd enjoyed when he'd been the gamekeeper at Shadowbrook Manor and she'd been a frequent visitor. He must have still been alive then but, perhaps like the Biddles, had obviously accepted that his master was...unusual.

Lucy sat beside her grandmother, of course, and while they chatted happily, Lucy changed tension and dropped stitches. Lucy was definitely improving as a knitter, but I could tell her heart wasn't in it. After a while, Agnes quietly slipped her knitting into Lucy's hands and Lucy's into hers. It was a lot like the way Lucy slipped her empty plate in front of Rafe and took his full one. I had to smile.

This was the first knitting club meeting since the kerfuffle over hosting the retreat, but all the vampires seemed to have come to accept that this thing was happening. So, instead of arguments about why we shouldn't have strangers knitting on the property, they never mentioned it at all and gossiped about people they knew, places they were thinking of going. The usual.

I enjoyed the late-night knitting much more having Lucy and Rafe there. And yet I also felt that they, particularly Lucy, were the outsiders. I might not be a local, but I was beginning to understand the ways of the local vampires, at least a little bit.

Since they were all on their best behavior, I announced the dates of our knitting and crochet retreat. I thought anybody who had a trip planned or reasons to be elsewhere might make sure to do it during that week. Svanhilde, who'd listened with her head on one side, said, "I would like to sign up for your knitting retreat, Guinevere. Is there room?"

The horror I felt cannot be described. I made an inarticulate sound, kind of a gasp and a choke all in one. Before I could dream up a response, Gryffyn Penrose rose smoothly to the occasion. "Svanhilde, think how humiliated the day walkers would be comparing your incredibly fine work with their rude efforts."

She tossed her long hair over her shoulder and put her hands on her hips. For a second, I could picture her on a warship heading out to battle or to conquer lands unknown or whatever she did in her Viking days. She said, "Then it is up to them to improve their work, surely."

He shook his head at her. "Unless they are undead, as we are, they can never hope to come close to your talent. Let the day walkers be."

She pouted her full red lips, but deep down she must know she'd be out of place. I suspected she'd only been trying to aggravate me anyway. Svanhilde was not a woman who evaded conflict. If anything she went out of her way to seek it. I would have to remember that. However, the matter was allowed to drop, and I shot Gryff a grateful look.

He said, "Perhaps, as it's getting towards the longest days of the year, you might contemplate a visit back to your homeland, Svanhilde."

She put down her knitting and said, "Bah. Norway in late May? It is full of fools playing tourist. I'd like to give them something to look at."

On these alarming words, she picked up her knitting and went back to it. She seemed to be knitting a blanket, or perhaps a shawl, in an intricate pattern. Her needles worked so rapidly and the work was so fine, I couldn't actually identify it.

I HAD another registration come through the Cornwall newsletter the next day. It was from a woman named Maggie Cooper. She put her experience down as advanced, her age was sixty-seven, and in the section that we'd left for comments, she said how nice it was to have a brand-new knitting retreat she could attend. Her comment made it seem as though she'd been to all the others, and there were quite a few. I suspected that none of us would have anything new to teach Maggie Cooper, but hopefully she just liked to sit in the company of other knitters and turn out amazing garments, a bit like the members of the vampire knitting club.

I was sharing this with Lucy when she said, "Huh, I had a similar comment from the very first person who signed up."

She pulled up her registration on her laptop, and we both peered at it. It was from Rosalind Wallace, who'd signed up hours after we announced the retreat. She was also an advanced knitter and in the comments had mentioned how excited she was about having a new knitting retreat to try in a location she hadn't yet visited.

We looked at each other. I said, "Well, that's good. At least we'll have two very experienced knitters. I wonder if they know each other?"

Lucy looked a bit glum. "I hope we get some newbies. I can't be the owner of a knitting shop and the worst knitter at the retreat. It would just be plain embarrassing."

I didn't really know what to say. It wasn't like Lucy didn't try. But even though I was her best friend, I couldn't pretend she was a great knitter when she so clearly wasn't. I thought it was a bit like being color-blind or something, just a very slight disability. I suspected she'd never become a proficient knitter. I think she suspected that, too.

With two months to go, we were well on our way to filling the retreat. I thought we had plenty of time to prepare. Mrs. Biddle, however, seemed to think two months wasn't nearly enough.

"There's so much to be done!" she cried. "Every room must be thoroughly cleaned and all the bedding brought out and washed and ironed..."

She went on and on, and I basically tuned her out. I caught snatches like making sure all the kettles were working in the bedrooms and bringing in fresh toiletries for all the bathrooms. I was sure there would be a bit of work, but I also thought she was making heavy weather of it. At one point I even said I would help her, and that got a snort of disbelief and a "No, thank you. I'll manage." She said it in a tone that made it clear she had no faith in my abilities to clean a room or make a bed.

I might have argued with her, but in fairness I wasn't particularly interested in doing either of those things, and if I did, no doubt she'd do nothing but criticize and remake the bed or reclean the room anyway. I figured with two months, she could manage to prepare eight bedrooms. She seemed to relish the fact that I'd be thrown out of mine since I lived in one of the nicest rooms in the house. I didn't care. I had brought few belongings with me and hadn't accumulated much more, so it would be easy to move into the apartment behind the kitchen.

I was sorry to see Lucy leave, but at least we'd organized the details and both felt confident we would run a successful first knitting retreat. Monday evening, before they left, we enjoyed a quiet evening—me, Lucy, Rafe, and Agnes, who would be as sad as I was when Lucy left. While we were chatting in the evening, we received another registration. Lily Tang was fifty and worked as an accountant in Birmingham. She put her ability as average. Whatever that meant.

Lucy and Rafe left on Tuesday morning quite early. I clung to Lucy when she was leaving. She hugged me back, but not in the needy way I was hanging on to her. She pulled back and said with understanding in her eyes, "You should come visit us in Oxford more often. You're always welcome. Now you have help with The Scallop Shell, you don't need to be there so much."

It was kind of her to say, but running the shop was my job, not a hobby I could pick up and put down. I needed to put down some roots if I was going to stay here, and that meant sticking around so those roots could take hold.

"I'll see you soon," I said.

She hugged me again, and I waved as she left.

As I watched Rafe's fancy black car head back toward Oxford, I didn't remember ever feeling quite so lonely.

However, I had a shop to run and a retreat to plan. That should keep me from getting maudlin.

CHAPTER 5

When I got into The Scallop Shell, I got busy opening up after our two closed days. I was thrilled that all but four of the spots for our knitting retreat were filled. Apart from a slight nervousness that Svanhilde would show up on the first day and claim she had booked a place in the class, which I wouldn't put past her, I was delighted with our results.

I was checking stock and getting an order ready when the door opened only ten minutes after we'd opened. I glanced up to see Agatha Trevellen, the owner of The Cornish Teapot. She'd been in a couple of times before. I knew she was a knitter but not a particularly regular one. I put down my order book and smiled at her. I liked Agatha and spent a fair bit of time in The Cornish Teapot. They had wonderful cakes, and it was a great place to sit and have a cup of tea and read a book or chat with the locals. I was trying my best to get to know my new neighbors.

"Agatha," I said with pleasure. "How nice to see you."

If she was a stranger, I might have jumped in with "How

can I help you?" But since it was Agatha, I suspected she'd come to gossip or tell me some local news. Like all villages, Tregrebi thrived on gossip, and normally anything that was worth knowing was passed around from ear to ear long before it showed up in our local newspaper.

I leaned on the desk and looked at her eagerly, waiting to hear the latest. Instead she surprised me by asking if there was any room left in the knitting retreat. I imagined she had a friend who knitted and was doubly pleased that I'd put a sign in the window. "We have four places left," I said, not without pride. I'd been worried we'd have no takers, and now we were nearly full only a few days after we'd announced it.

She looked the tiniest bit sheepish, I thought, and then said, "I was wondering if I might book one of those places."

To say I was shocked was an understatement. "You want to come to a knitting retreat in your own hometown?" It wasn't just that, it was the fact that I now knew that Mrs. Biddle and she had a rivalry going. What the housekeeper would say if she knew that Agatha Trevellen was going to be partaking of her Cornish afternoon teas every day, I shuddered to think.

Perhaps that was on Agatha's mind, too, because she said, "I'd dearly love to improve my knitting skills. When winter comes and the rains set in, there's nothing nicer than cozying up by the fire with your knitting. The trouble is, I feel that I could knit so much better. I'd so like to improve."

I opened my mouth, but before I could speak, she went on. "Now I've already talked to Claire, and she's willing to run The Teapot for me for a week, so you see, I'll have the time." Claire was her daughter and one of the first friends I'd made here in Tregrebi.

What could I say? I couldn't tell her she couldn't come when I'd just disclosed that I had spaces left. I suspected there might be trouble ahead, but I comforted myself with the knowledge that I'd rather have Agatha Trevellen in my knitting retreat than Svanhilde.

"Would it be all right if I don't stay in the house? I'd prefer to sleep in my own bed."

I didn't think that would be a problem. I told her I'd work out the discount and let her know, but in the back of my mind I thought I could add an extra guest if she didn't need to stay at Shadowbrook. Also, if she didn't stay over, there was less for Mrs. Biddle to grumble about.

So, with what enthusiasm I could muster, I said how thrilled I was. Really, I was. At least Agatha was a local and someone I already knew. Apart from facing the wrath of Mrs. Biddle, I thought Agatha would be a really good addition to the group. She filled out the form right there and paid the deposit and even bought a kit for a cushion cover. With a smile at me, she said, "I've got two months to get my skills up. I'll try not to embarrass myself."

"It's for all levels," I assured her. "And you'll be able to tell the other participants about local places to go and so on. I'm really happy you're coming."

She looked delighted as she left, and I only hoped I was right and Mrs. Biddle would be too busy running around making beds and serving tea to worry that her rival was in the house.

The last spots were quickly filled. A man of twenty-seven named Elliot Thomas signed up. He put his proficiency as reasonable and in the information box said he was a clothing designer and interested in incorporating knitting and crochet into his clothing designs. I thought this was really cool. So far Elliot was the only man in the group, but he must have expected that.

I was delighted to see that both Elliot and Maggie Cooper tagged my shop and Lucy's in their Instagram feeds and said how much they were looking forward to the retreat. We'd definitely encouraged people to share the retreat on social media, and it was great to see news of the retreat online.

Then a man named Nigel Hargreaves phoned me and asked a few questions about the retreat. He sounded sad, as he said that he used to attend knitting retreats with his wife, but now he'd be coming alone for the first time. My heart went out to him, and I told him that he wouldn't be the only man, which cheered him up, and that we had people of all ages and abilities. He asked about sharing a room, as had Elliot, so it was natural to put them together.

The last spot was taken by Isabel Sterling. She said she was a beginning knitter but keen to learn. She was twenty-eight. I thought it was nice that we had such a range of ages.

I was going to send Lucy an email and tell her we got to ten, but I was too excited, so I phoned her instead. We did the phone equivalent of a high five, and she told me how happy she was that we'd be working together and praised me again for coming up with such a great idea. I was the first one to admit that there was nothing startling about a knit-ting retreat. It wasn't like I'd invented it. Still, it was defi-nitely a way for both of us, not only to spend some time together, but market our two businesses in a fun and different way.

I told her that with Agatha not staying at Shadowbrook, and Elliot and Nigel sharing a room, we had been able to add a tenth person. We were now full, and I happily added a Sold Out banner to the website.

The two months went surprisingly quickly. Apart from running the shop and taking every invitation that was offered to me as I tried to get more entrenched in the community, I mostly just worked on the retreat.

When Andrew Jackson invited me to his house, I was particularly thrilled. It was the night of the full moon, and he specified that I wear a robe, so I wasn't surprised when I arrived at his cottage to find that he'd clearly planned a cere- mony. His cottage was beautiful and sat alone on a rocky promontory overlooking the ocean. He also had no neigh- bors, which I was certain was one of the reasons he'd bought it. As I walked up the path, two ravens circled overhead and cawed at me. I was pretty sure they were the ravens who talked to Andrew. He called them Huginn and Muninn, after the Norse ravens who brought news to Odin. I thought they were his familiars but also newsgatherers.

Andrew greeted me warmly and invited me inside. His cottage was cozy inside, with comfortable furniture and a fire crackling in the grate. He ran a bookstore, and his love of books spilled into his home. Two walls of the main room were taken up with bookshelves, where I glimpsed books on everything from the meaning of crystals to the latest thriller.

A couple of people were already there, and he introduced me. No need to tell me they were witches; it was obvious. A woman named Eliza, with braided ash-blond hair and pale blue eyes, greeted me warmly. I was clearly the newcomer in the group. She said she'd driven over from a nearby village, where she ran a pharmacy. She introduced me to Marcus, his wild, tangled locks framing a broad face. He was around my age and greeted me with a distinctly Cornish accent. "I'm a plumber by trade if you're ever in need of one," he told me. He noted my accent, and as I was explaining how I'd come to live in Cornwall, there was a knock on the door and Andrew opened it to let in Ewan.

I hadn't seen Ewan for some time, but he was unforgettable with his shoulder-length brown hair, his clear gray eyes, and the sense of calm that he projected. He kept an eye on St. Jerome's Well, a sacred spot not far from here. I'd thought of him as very much a lone witch, so was surprised to see him at the gathering of a coven. After greeting Andrew, he came toward me. "Jennifer," he said. "It's nice to see you again."

He greeted the other witches, so he was obviously not as solitary as I'd imagined.

One more person came to the door. Her name was Luna, and she was the oldest among us, with long white hair and the kindest face I'd ever seen. As she clasped my hands, her silver bracelets tinkled.

Andrew was a wonderful host, soon ushering us into his dining room, where he'd laid out a buffet supper. "I thought we'd eat first and head outside when the moon's risen a little higher," he said.

We dined on cold meats and salads. There was no alcohol but a variety of herbal teas, fresh water, and soft drinks. I had a delicious tea that included rosehips, ginger, and apple.

I sat beside Ewan as we ate, and he told me he was writing a book about the mystical history of Cornwall. We were talking about ley lines when Andrew called us all to order and asked us to head outside. He wrapped himself in an emerald-green robe and lifted an athame, his sacred dagger, from the mantel.

A few of the others donned their own robes, but all I had with me was a long, knitted sweater that Agnes had made for me when she heard I was going to be out on a windy hillside at night. It was midnight blue, and she'd added a hood for extra warmth. It might not be a classic robe, but I would be warm.

The rugged cliffs of Cornwall loomed stark against the night sky as we followed Andrew to his sacred spot, the sea below churning as if whispering secrets to the moon. As he set the stage for tonight's ceremony, his robe fluttered in the brisk wind, the fabric whispering against the ancient stones.

Near the circle's edge, Huginn and Muninn, Andrew's familiars, perched solemnly on a gnarled piece of driftwood, their eyes like liquid obsidian as they stared at us.

When we'd gathered, Andrew began to cast the circle with salt and moonstone, creating a sanctuary of power on the cliffs edge. Eliza, with her braided ash-blond hair and pale blue eyes, wore a robe the color of fresh snow. Marcus, his wild hair tossing, wore a robe of earthy browns stitched with patterns of leaves and roots. Luna wore black, startling against her white hair. Ewan, like me, had no ceremonial robe, but donned a well-worn gray woolen coat with an orange scarf knotted around his throat.

Andrew took his place at the altar, a simple wooden table covered with a cloth of deep purple held in place by large crystals. In the center was a large, ornate chalice filled with moon water.

Raising his arms, Andrew began the incantation, his voice strong against the wind. "By the light of the full moon, we gather. By the ebb and flow of the tide, we align. Spirits of air, earth, fire, and water converge here upon this sacred site.

Moon above, sea below, bless us with your glowing light. Guide us in our rites tonight."

I could feel our collective energy and power as he continued, and then Andrew drew his athame, directing the power towards the moon. "Great Luna, your children call to you. Accept our energies, our desires, our thanks."

The ravens cawed, a stark, echoing sound that seemed to reach beyond the cliffs, beyond the night. He called, "We release what no longer serves, embrace the blessings yet to come."

As the ceremony drew to a close, we joined hands, standing in a circle together. Andrew chanted, "As the moon wanes, so shall our fears. As the moon waxes, so shall our courage. Blessed be."

"Blessed be," we all chorused.

As we headed back toward the cottage, I dropped back a little, enjoying the feeling of connection with my fellow witches and the energy of the moon. Then my reverie was broken as the two ravens circled me, crying out. I was so startled, I stumbled and nearly fell. Andrew was behind me and came to grab my arm, though I'd already righted myself.

He didn't say anything, but a cold feeling squeezed my heart. The two ravens now settled, one on each of Andrew's shoulders, and it seemed like they were whispering to him.

"What is it?" I asked him.

He patted me awkwardly, given that he had a raven on either shoulder. "The trouble with ravens is that they're gloomy creatures, always looking on the dark side. They're telling me they see death in your future, but they always see death."

Even though he kept his voice light and cheerful, I felt

that he was taking the birds more seriously than he was letting on. "Death?" I nearly shrieked. I scanned through my mind of everybody I knew and loved. Some of them were already undead, so I didn't need to worry about them, but there were my parents and my friends at home. I still had three living grandparents, but they were obviously getting on in age. I'd make sure to phone my folks as soon as I got home and make sure everything was okay.

As I was leaving, Andrew said, "One minute, Jennifer." He waited until everyone had gone and then said, "I have something for you." And he reached out and slipped a bracelet around my wrist. It was silver and engraved with symbols. He kept his hand over my wrist and took mine and put it atop his, and then he did a protection spell.

"Circle of silver, guard this sister,
Reflect all ill, let harm be none.
Symbols with power strong,
Shield from darkness and from wrong.
By moon's light and star's embrace,
Secure within this sacred space.
Let this band be a fortress sure,
Against all that's dark and impure.
As I will it, so mote it be,
Wrapped in safety, forever free."

As I walked out of his front door and down the flagstone path that he'd lit with flaming torches, I heard the cry of a raven and then the lights went out behind me. A great gust of wind came up and blew out all the torches at once, as though someone had turned off a celestial light switch and plunged me into darkness.

I got home as quickly as I could, but as I entered Shadowbrook Manor, a shiver crawled up the back of my spine, and I'd have been quite happy to have Gryff Penrose standing in the middle of the living room, but of course the one time I actually wanted him, he wasn't there. No one was there. The Biddles were obviously in their own cottage, and I had Shadowbrook Manor all to myself. No doubt I'd cause havoc to the electric bill, but I didn't care as I turned on every light in the place. Then I called my parents. It was early evening in Boston and it was wonderful to hear my mom sounding perfectly normal and passing on all the gossip about what was going on at home.

When I got off the phone, I looked down at the bracelet around my wrist. I wasn't alone, I reminded myself. Andrew Jackson was not only another witch, but he was my friend. And I'd been invited to join a local coven.

Those ravens had spooked me, that was all. I was so happy that instead of a cawing bird for my familiar, I had a particularly fluffy cat. And as though I had conjured her, I heard Busby meowing at the window. I opened it, and she jumped inside and rubbed against me. And then she sat on my bed as I got undressed. I got ready for bed and took off all my jewelry, but I left the protection amulet around my wrist.

I was not going to discount the warning of two ravens.

CHAPTER 6

I always think that an enterprise that starts on a sunny day ought to be blessed with good fortune. It's a foolish notion, and to somebody who grew up in Boston, where lots of enterprises began with rain or snow or fog, it was a bit silly, but the day that we were expecting everybody to our knitting and crochet retreat dawned without a cloud in the sky.

I fell in love with Shadowbrook Manor the first time I saw it; it's beautiful and historic and overlooks the ocean and very pretty gardens. Even the supposedly abandoned tin mine is picturesque, with its old chimney pointing skyward. But that morning, not only was the sun shining, but the manor house interior was gleaming. It was like having sunshine both outside and in. Mrs. Biddle and I might have our differences, but I could not deny that the woman was a fine housekeeper. Every surface glowed, and there was a faint smell of lemon and beeswax in the air where she'd polished everything from the grandfather clock to the most insignificant side table. The rugs were freshly vacuumed, the windows sparkled from their recent cleaning, and beautiful bouquets of flowers filled every room. I'd peeped into each of the guestrooms and knew that if I were walking into one of them, I'd have been delighted. They each had their own character, pretty linens, a fresh carafe of water on each bedside. The kettles that Mrs. Biddle had been so worried about sat, one in each room, on a tray with a doily and an assortment of tea bags, and where other bed and breakfasts might offer a couple of cookies in a cellophane packet, Mrs. Biddle had a little plate of her homemade shortbread covered in cling film, as she called it, with a handwritten note saying these biscuits were handmade in Cornwall and listing the ingredients. It was such a nice touch.

Lucy was the first to arrive, thank goodness, having left Oxford at the crack of dawn. She'd driven herself, and when her little red car pulled up, I threw open the front door to welcome her. We hugged and both started talking at once.

Like me, she was lavish in her praise to Mrs. Biddle for how nice everything looked. We had left check-in time flexible, as people were coming from all over.

The manager's suite, where she and I were staying, had an outside entrance and could also be reached through the kitchen. Since Mrs. Biddle was busy preparing a lot of meals for a lot of guests, Lucy and I naturally were too terrified to go into the kitchen. We unpacked her stuff from her car and carried it into the suite's front door, a modest affair tucked around the side of the manor house. Lucy was going to move her car into the big garage, but Mr. Biddle arrived (after we'd finished unpacking the car) and said he'd put the vehicle away.

He drove off, and we hauled Lucy's suitcase, a case full of

knitting supplies she'd thought she might need, and her knitting bag into our temporary quarters.

The apartment was great, with two bedrooms and its own living room and study, complete with desk, computer, printer and a proper business phone, because of course the people who ran the bed and breakfast had done the bookings and billing and so on in here, so there was a full setup.

I insisted Lucy take the larger bedroom with the en suite. I was just as happy with the smaller of the two rooms, and since I'd already moved my things into it, there wasn't much point in her arguing. There was a second bathroom I could use. The suite didn't have a full kitchen, as it was adjacent to the main cooking area, but there was a kitchenette with a small fridge, and it was perfect for making our own coffee and tea and keeping snacks. Mrs. Biddle had even given us the full homemade shortbread cookie treatment, and inside the small fridge were water and milk for our hot drinks.

"I'm hungry," Lucy said after she'd finished unpacking. It was nearly one o'clock, and we'd moved into the main house, ready for guests to arrive. I had my knitting with me. Lucy had a tablet computer with the week's schedule.

I was too scared to go into the kitchen and tell Mrs. Biddle we wanted lunch, but luckily, she stomped out and said, "I suppose you'll be wanting lunch."

"If it's not too much trouble," Lucy said.

Mrs. Biddle looked as though she was on the brink of telling Lucy it was far too much trouble but perhaps remembered that she was married to Rafe, who paid their salary. Instead she said, "You'll have to eat it in the kitchen. I'll not have you two messing up my clean rooms."

"The kitchen is fine," we said in unison.

She called us in a few minutes later, and we sat at the kitchen table with a pot of tea and an assortment of the sandwiches that she would no doubt be serving for afternoon tea in the days to come.

While we ate, she ignored us, making and baking the shortbread cookies she'd placed in all the rooms. The kitchen smelled amazing.

Mr. Biddle appeared at the kitchen door, and she passed him a mug of tea and a plate of sandwiches on what looked like a cracked plate. He glanced longingly at us sitting around the nice table but was clearly too cowed by his disapproving wife to enter the kitchen. Instead he nodded at us and humbly took his meal to sit outside.

When we'd finished, Lucy said we should take advantage of the fact that Mrs. Biddle had cleaned Shadowbrook Manor from top to bottom and do a cleansing of old energies. She pulled from her pack a carefully-wrapped stick of sage. I told her that while she was cleansing the energy inside, I'd put a protection spell around the manor house.

We headed off immediately to our tasks. I used salt that I'd purified under the light of a full moon. I visualized the salt as a powerful energy field keeping everyone within it safe. As I sprinkled the salt around the perimeter of the house, I said,

"Spirits of the north, south, east and west,
hear my request.
Cloak this retreat in safety and calm.
Across this threshold, let only love and joy preside,
inside these walls, peace and creativity abide.
So I will, so mote it be."

I felt much lighter after we'd done our tasks. We headed back to the living room and chatted. It was so nice to catch up. I glanced up at one point, thinking I saw our first guest arriving, but it was Mrs. Biddle outside with a broom. I ran to the door and opened it. She looked very put out. "I'll need to have a word with that fool husband of mine. He's chucked a load of salt all over my nice clean entryway. Does the great *tuss* think we're in danger of ice and snow in May?"

She was sweeping energetically, and I could see the salt I'd sprinkled across the doorway scattering to the winds.

There was no time to replace it, and even if I did, the sharp-eyed housekeeper would only disperse it again.

Half an hour later, the front doorbell rang, signifying our first guest had arrived.

"It's so exciting," Lucy said, a smile blooming.

We both headed toward the front foyer, but Mrs. Biddle was there before us.

The first person to arrive was, not surprisingly, Agatha Trevellen, since she lived locally. However, as pleased as I was to see her, I could have wished that she'd come later, maybe in a bunch so she wouldn't be quite so obviously noticed.

I hadn't actually mentioned to Mrs. Biddle that Agatha would be joining us. I didn't think it was her business, and I didn't need two months of arguments, so when Mrs. Biddle opened the door to Agatha Trevellen, who was standing there with a knitting bag in her hands. The housekeeper asked, "And what might you be doing here?"

Not exactly the rousing welcome I'd been hoping for. Lucy and I both rushed forward. "Agatha, I'm so pleased you could make it," I said.

She'd met Lucy, of course, at our opening for The Scallop Shell, and Lucy greeted her like they were the best of dear old friends. That shut Mrs. Biddle up, so she merely gave a sniff, left the door wide open, and turned around and stomped back to her kitchen.

"Come in," I said, as though Mrs. Biddle hadn't just put on the rudest performance of a door greeter possibly ever.

Agatha walked in and said, "Oh dear, Mrs. Biddle doesn't seem too pleased."

"I think she was just surprised," Lucy assured her.

Her eyes twinkled at me. "You didn't tell her I was coming, did you?"

"In fairness, I didn't tell her the names of anyone who was coming."

She gazed around her as though drinking the place in. "Ever since Mrs. Biddle's worked here, I've never been allowed to set foot across the threshold."

"Well, come in," Lucy said. She followed us and turned a slow circle in the big living room with those picture windows and the French doors leading to a veranda and the sea views.

"What a beautiful room." She was just as complimentary about the dining room. It did look particularly fine, with the table already set and a huge vase of fresh flowers as its centerpiece. Even though it wasn't my house, I admit I felt pride in how nice everything looked.

"I hope I'm not too early, but the opening time did say three o'clock, and I like to be early."

"We're starting with a meet and greet for everyone to get to know each other," Lucy explained. "Mrs. Biddle is making her famous shortbread cookies."

She chuckled. "It's a good thing you didn't tell her I was coming, or I would fear that my shortbread might be laced with poison."

We both laughed, but it was a reedy sound. I put my hand

on my protection bracelet, which I'd been wearing pretty much full-time since Andrew gave it to me. I noticed Lucy touched an amulet she wore around her neck. The beautiful ruby ring that had belonged to her grandmother glowed briefly on the middle finger of her left hand, and beside it were the wedding and engagement rings bestowed on her by Rafe. I thought if ever there was a woman who was protected, it was Lucy. As long as I stayed close to her side, I didn't think much could happen to me either.

At least I hoped so. Why had those ravens put the idea of death into my head? I tried not to think about it, but at odd times, like late at night when the sea was churning outside my window and the old house creaked and groaned, I'd imagine the crows cackling as some horrible fate befell me.

CHAPTER 7

The next time the doorbell rang, I ran to get there before Mrs. Biddle could insult another of our guests. Anthea Fitzgerald stood there, dressed as though she'd pulled things out of the ironing basket and not bothered to iron them. I got that she passionately cared about the environment and wearing natural fabrics, but did everything have to look like it had barely stopped being a weed?

Behind her large glasses, her pale blue eyes widened in surprise, as though she hadn't expected to find me here, even though I was the one running the retreat. "Oh, Jennifer," she said in that breathless way of hers. Then she glanced behind her. Was she thinking about leaving before she got here? Frankly, if she did, I didn't think I'd stop her.

Then once more Lucy was at my side. "Anthea, I'm so glad you could make it. How was your trip down?"

Anthea then explained that because of the carbon footprint, she'd taken trains and buses from the Lake District all the way to Cornwall. Her description of her trip was boring, if eco-friendly.

I told her I'd show her to her room. We'd set our pricing so that the smallest rooms were cheaper and the larger, more elaborate rooms more expensive. Room 1, which I usually lived in, was the priciest, and Beatrice Huntington-Cole had chosen that one.

All our linens were Egyptian cotton with a crazy high thread count, and even though I'd given Anthea the simplest room, I saw her walk over and test the comforter and turn up her nose. The thing was, I didn't mind that she was so eco-friendly, but she acted as though she were a superior being to everyone else, and that just got to me. The upstairs rooms were four to each side of a long corridor, with two bathrooms at the end of the hall, shared by the four rooms at that end of the hall. The rest of the rooms were en suite.

When Anthea came downstairs, she sat making uneasy small talk with Agatha, and then we had another arrival.

A woman named Rosalind Wallace showed up next. If I could have described her in one word, it would have been "grandmother." She had a kindly face and a big bosom and rounded figure that was made for cuddles and hugs. She'd already told us she was a proficient knitter, but outside of garments crafted by the vampires, who'd been perfecting their craft for hundreds of years, she was probably wearing the most beautifully-knit garment I'd ever seen.

Even her knitting bag was hand-knit and quite a showpiece.

I took a look at the ensemble and said, "If you made those yourself, I don't think there's anything we can teach you here."

She was wearing a classic Chanel-style jacket with a knit skirt and sensible black walking shoes. However, she seemed absolutely delighted to be here. She immediately compli-mented me on starting a new retreat.

"I go to as many of them as I can, but to come to Cornwall, where I used to holiday as a girl, is such a treat." And then, as we dragged in her case for her, she glanced around, and as most people did, her gaze went straight through to the lounge with its large windows and ocean view. "What a lovely home," she said.

I thought that was such a nice way to put it, because while it had been run for some years as a bed and breakfast, at its heart it had been built as a home, and I suspected one day Rafe and Lucy would turn it back into that. But for now, it would be a home away from home for ten knitters from budding to experienced.

She nodded in a friendly way to the women already chat-ting away in the living room, and then Lucy and I would both have taken her upstairs, except the doorbell rang again, and Lucy went to answer it. An older woman's voice could clearly be heard from the front door saying, "What a beautiful home. I'm Maggie Cooper, here for the knitting retreat."

Rosalind Wallace jerked as though I had plucked the knitting needle that was visible from her knitting bag and poked her with it. Her whole body stiffened, and she turned with a gaze of consternation—I think that would be the closest word. And then as quickly as it had come, the expres-sion went, and she was all pleasantness and smiles walking back down the two stairs we'd already traveled.

By this time, Maggie Cooper had come all the way inside. As she glanced around, obviously ready to praise the hallway, she caught sight of Rosalind and went through a similar transformation from chagrin to delight. I suspected that the chagrin was the true feeling and the delight was the fake one papered on top of it.

"Why, Rosalind, how delightful to see you again."

The two went towards each other and embraced like the dearest of friends, but I had seen the looks of horror that each had let show, however briefly.

Rosalind chuckled. "Maggie and I have spent many a knitting retreat in each other's company. How many is it now?"

Maggie shook her head. She was built on much slimmer lines than Rosalind, with iron-gray hair that she wore in a short bob, a tartan skirt and with it, a red sweater that was equally as spectacular as the one Rosalind was wearing. I thought about the way they had greeted each other, and the word "rivalry" crossed my mind. These two would clearly be the most experienced knitters in the bunch. I wondered how often they'd ended up on the same retreats and wished they hadn't. Perhaps each of them was used to being the most amazing knitter in the room and to have to share that glory was difficult. I was guessing like crazy, but something was between them. I glanced at Lucy. I was sure she'd felt it too.

Then Rosalind said, "It's my grandson's birthday coming up, and he so loves my sweaters. It's such a joy to knit for grandchildren. What a shame you never had any."

Ouch. I never had children, at least not yet, and I was already being pressured by my mother to give her some grandchildren. I knew how disappointed she'd be if I let her down. So for one grandmother to offer fake sympathy to a woman her age who didn't have any grandchildren seemed cruel.

But Maggie Cooper didn't even flinch. She smiled and

said, "I've plenty of nieces and nephews and great-nieces and -nephews to knit for. And, of course, not having children allowed me to enjoy a fulfilling and prestigious career."

Oh my gosh, and the battle lines were drawn. We'd barely started, and I had a feeling it was going to be a very interesting week. I led Rosalind to her room while Lucy took Maggie to hers. Fortunately, they were at opposite ends of the corridor from each other. Maggie had Room 2, next to the turret room. Rosalind had Room 5, across the hall from Anthea.

The next person to arrive was Sunita Rai, who had described herself as a burned-out financial analyst from London who loved to crochet for stress relief. She wore comfortable jeans and a navy blue T-shirt. She looked delighted to meet us and said how much she'd been looking forward to this.

"I like to design my own garments," she said to both of us as though this was some kind of an interview. "I was born in Nepal, and I love to use the colors and designs of my youth and my work, but my proficiency isn't as good as I'd like. So, I'm here both to learn better technique and also just to relax by the ocean and recharge."

I assured her that we had set up this retreat to leave plenty of time for people to nap or walk on the beach or, if they wanted to get on with it, sit and knit or crochet.

She nodded. "Yes, I looked at the way you've set up the schedule, and I liked that I could be as relaxed as I wanted or work as hard as I decide to. I think I shall take each day as it comes."

I laughed. "I think that's a great way for all of us to live our lives."

Unlike everybody else, she barely gave the other guests a glance but said, "If you'll show me to my room, I've a few emails I have yet to send before I can relax." And then a slightly alarmed look crossed her face. "You do have Wi-Fi in the bedrooms, don't you?"

I assured her that we did and really hoped that Sunita didn't spend most of the week putting out work fires. I'd had that kind of job myself, and I remembered how often my weekends and supposed vacations had been intruded on by work. I didn't miss those days. Maybe I didn't make as much money as I had in Boston, but I lived in a beautiful place and made my living around something I truly loved. I was not going to complain.

Within half an hour, everyone who had arrived was sitting in the main room. Rosalind wasted no time in pulling out a partly knitted sweater from her bag and industriously setting to work on it. Not to be outdone, Maggie Cooper pulled out her own piece of work.

I couldn't quite figure out what it was, and she must have caught my puzzled look, for she said, "It's going to be a beret. I've designed it myself, using the same design as my sweater." Now I realized the red wool of the beret was the same red in her sweater. "It's from a Finnish pattern, but the design is all my own." She sounded rather pleased with herself, and who could blame her?

Rosalind knit even more quickly. The only people I'd ever seen knit faster than Rosalind Wallace were undead ones. She said, "I do think we can overcomplicate things. Sometimes simplest is best."

I couldn't help glancing at her Chanel-style jacket, which was one of the most complicated pieces of knitting I'd ever seen, but I wisely kept my mouth shut. Luckily, so did Maggie Cooper.

Agatha Trevellen laughed and said, "You make me feel quite lazy. I wasn't planning to start knitting until tomorrow."

Rosalind replied, "My mother always used to say idle hands are the devil's workshop. I'm not sure that's true, but the habits of a lifetime are hard to break. I find if I sit down and don't have a piece of work in my hands, I feel quite peculiar."

Maggie Cooper nodded. "Once I retired, I felt the same way."

"What kind of work did you do?" Agatha wanted to know.

A look of annoyance passed over Rosalind Wallace's face, but Maggie Cooper looked delighted by the question. "I was a librarian, dear, in a very prestigious private library in London. Oh, the stories I could tell you. But naturally, one learns discretion."

"You lived in London?" Agatha continued, politely.

"I did. My husband was a barrister and, latterly, a magistrate, so we lived in London. I sadly lost him several years ago, and so I moved to Bath, which still has culture and theater and so on, but at a slower pace."

The doorbell announced another arrival, and Lucy and I both jumped up and headed to the door. The woman standing on the doorstep immediately made me feel dowdy. She was just so glamorous.

"Good afternoon," she said in a well-modulated tone that spoke of finishing schools and garden parties. "I'm Beatrice Huntington-Cole."

Of course this was Beatrice Huntington-Cole, with her double-barreled last name and wearing a gorgeous dark green coat, black trousers, and shoes bearing the Chanel logo. She appeared to be around sixty. Her jewelry was exquisite, and there was plenty of it. In fact, everything about her whispered of wealth. She swept in and held out her hands.

"You must be Jennifer. I recognize your picture from your website. How lovely to meet you." Somehow she'd gone from being the greetee to the greeter. Then she turned to Lucy and said she recognized her as well. "I'm so very pleased to be here. I used to come to Cornwall as a girl. I've always loved it." Then her eyes clouded with sadness. "I lost my husband recently, you see. I felt I needed something to take my mind off my grief."

"I'm so sorry," we both said at the same time.

She gave a misty smile and then looked about. I felt like she was looking for the bellhop or the porter to take her two large cases upstairs for her. Since I didn't imagine Mr. Biddle was going to oblige, I grabbed one and Lucy grabbed the other, and we said we'd show her to her room. Even though she'd booked the nicest room, I was worried she'd think it below the standard she was accustomed to. Number 1 was the room that I usually stayed in and was by far the grandest of the guest rooms, with its balcony overlooking the ocean and its own turret with a spiral staircase and a round room that I used as an office and reading nook.

When she entered it, she glanced around and said, "Oh, how pretty."

No doubt she was accustomed to staying at the Ritz, but I felt she could have done a bit better than "Oh, how pretty." Still, at least she wasn't complaining. As we had with the others, we left her to unpack and told her we'd meet her downstairs.

It didn't take her long to freshen up, and when she came back down, she was wearing the same black trousers with a cashmere sweater that I did not think she had knit herself. It was gorgeous, though. From her perfectly-coiffed frosted blond hair to the elegant face that I suspected was not a stranger to some cosmetic enhancements and her slim, toned figure, she looked as though she'd be more at home in a receiving line welcoming her guests to some fancy ball than sitting here in Cornwall on a knitting retreat. However, she was pleasant enough, and I could see she was making an effort to remember each person's name as she was introduced. She smiled at Maggie and Rosalind, who were probably close to her in age but looked unfashionable, even dowdy by comparison.

"What lovely work," she said, leaning closer to Maggie.

The retired librarian was happy to explain once more about the beret she had designed herself. "Since I retired and then was widowed, I've needed something to keep my hands and my brain occupied."

A shadow of sadness crossed Beatrice's face. Impulsively she leaned forward and rubbed Maggie Cooper's upper arm in a comforting way. "I'm so very sorry to hear that. I, too, recently lost my husband. I also have picked up knitting and crochet again to fill my time. It's the evenings that are so long, isn't it?"

Maggie Cooper nodded and sighed, and her knitting sat forgotten in her lap as the two spoke in low voices about their loss. I wasn't trying to eavesdrop, but Agatha had begun talking to Rosalind, and as I was closer to Maggie and Beatrice and they weren't particularly trying to keep their voices low, it was impossible not to hear. Maggie's barrister had died of a massive coronary. She shook her head.

"He'd finished his work for the day but hadn't even taken off his robes. Collapsed in chambers. Even his wig was still on. It was a terrible shock for me, but I know it was how he would have wanted to go."

Beatrice patted her new friend's hand. "My husband died at home after a brief and severe illness, which didn't seem any more serious than the flu, and then it turned into pneumonia." Beatrice's voice faded, and she reached up with one perfectly manicured finger to dab at the corner of her eye.

From there they moved on to stories of how they were coping and the things people had said, both the helpful and the wildly inappropriate.

The next time the doorbell rang, it was a young man and a young woman standing there. Since we only had two men registered, and one had mentioned he'd recently graduated from a fashion college in London, I took a wild guess. "Elliot?"

He laughed. He was a good-looking guy, boyish and open-faced. "Pleased to meet you," he said. And then he turned to his companion, who looked a bit uncomfortable standing there on the doorstep beside him. "And this is Issy. I saw her waiting at the bus stop with her knitting bag and took a guess that she was on her way here, so I gave her a lift."

Was he making it absolutely clear they weren't a couple?

Isabel Sterling wore her long, dark hair straight, hanging nearly to her waist. She had almond-shaped eyes that were gray-green in color, and a pointed chin. She was very pretty but had an anxious energy about her. Her hands fluttered nervously when she reminded me that she was just learning how to knit, and I could see that her fingernails were bitten to the quick.

She wore tight jeans and a sweatshirt emblazoned with Keep Calm and Smash the Patriarchy. I took a wild guess that Isabel Sterling was a feminist.

Whatever, we greeted both of them and showed them to their rooms. Elliot would be sharing with a man called Nigel Hargreaves, who'd mentioned he was retired in his comments. No doubt there'd be quite an age difference.

"Do you prefer Isabel or Issy?" I asked as I walked her farther down the corridor to her room, beside Rosalind Wallace's.

"I don't mind either. Most people call me Issy."

"Then I will, too," I said with a smile. "I like your sweatshirt."

She glanced down as though she couldn't remember what she had on. "Thanks. Mum bought it for me."

I left her to unpack and headed back toward the stairway downstairs. Elliot popped his head out of the room. "Does it matter which bed I have?" He and Nigel were the only two sharing a room, as Agatha Trevellen would go home to sleep in her own bed, though she'd be here for breakfast every morning and had said she wanted to join in all the evening meals as well.

I thought about Nigel being older and suggested he give the older man the bed closest to the bathroom, as he'd no doubt be visiting it during the night.

Lily Tang arrived soon after, saying she'd been caught in traffic driving down from Birmingham. I assured her she was in plenty of time. She wore a hand-knit Fair Isle vest over a white shirt with dark trousers and loafers. Her dark hair was bobbed, and her eyeglasses were as much a fashion state-ment as a way to correct her vision. She was quick to rave about the view, and when I showed her to her room, she rushed to the window and opened it. "Oh, I love the sea air. It smells so good. And the view is to die for." I was glad she'd ended up with an ocean view.

Soon, everyone but Nigel Hargreaves was gathered in the spacious living room, and I felt as though the house grew happier being filled with people and voices after so long.

Mrs. Biddle came in with tea and more of her homemade cookies. Biscuits, as she called them.

"I could do coffee, if you prefer," she said in the kind of voice that suggested she'd like to do anything but. No one was foolish enough to ask for coffee, and soon we were sitting around drinking tea and munching her definitely delicious shortbread as we talked about the one thing we all had in common, and that was knitting and crochet.

Anthea stopped talking about her shop and said to Mrs. Biddle, "Are any of those vegan?"

Mrs. Biddle all but dropped the plate of biscuits on the floor. "Vegan?" she nearly shouted.

Anthea looked quite surprised and glanced from Mrs. Biddle to Lucy and me. "Surely Lucy and Jennifer told you? I'm vegan and gluten-free."

Mrs. Biddle repeated in an astonished tone. "Vegan? *And* gluten-free? At the same time?" Then she turned to glare at me. "No, I was not informed that we had someone who was vegan and gluten-free." Then she appealed to the room huffily. "How am I to make a scone without butter or flour? And I suppose you can't eat Cornish clotted cream?"

Anthea put a hand to her spare chest. "I couldn't."

"Well, I never."

"Anthea, you didn't put any of this on your intake form." I'd been careful to ask about dietary preferences.

She looked hurt. "I thought you'd remember." I could not believe she was trying to blame me. If I'd thought about it, I probably did know she was vegan, but I'd trusted what people wrote on their forms, and she'd said nothing about her food preferences.

At this point, Agatha Trevellen spoke up. "I've got some vegan and gluten-free items at The Cornish Teapot. I'm sure I could provide enough for your afternoon teas, Anthea."

Once more, Mrs. Biddle looked to be in danger of dropping the plate of biscuits onto the floor. Her attitude changed from one of martyrdom to defender of her castle. "That won't be necessary. I will provide suitable substitutions. I just wish I'd been informed."

I felt completely aggrieved. When Mrs. Biddle had gone, I turned to Anthea. "Did you miss the spot on the form to mention any dietary requirements?"

Anthea blinked her wide blue eyes at me. "But we were in Oxford together. You must have remembered I was vegan and gluten-free."

In fact, I'd had plenty of other things on my mind in Oxford. I wasn't sure what I would have replied, but Lucy smoothly intervened. "We'll make it work, Anthea. At least now we know."

Instead of letting the subject drop, as she would have if she'd had a smidgen of tact, Anthea began to preach the virtues of her lifestyle. Then she pulled out a ball of wool that she smugly told us was made from organic flax. I had to admit it was beautiful. Even though I had to appreciate that she had her values and stuck to them, I thought she'd be a lot more likable if she let other people make their own choices and gave the preaching a rest.

What's more, I recalled what Margaret Twigg, the head of Lucy's coven in Oxford, had said about Anthea. She did not believe her practices were quite as pure as she made them out to be. I couldn't say it was comforting to think that the woman who was acting so holier-than-thou might be hiding a bit of a dark secret, but it helped.

CHAPTER 8

he doorbell rang once again as we were finishing our tea. Since Lucy had a mouth full of shortbread and was politely listening to Anthea talking about some of the marketing techniques she had begun implementing from the course we had taken in Oxford, I waved her back to her seat and jumped up to take care of the new arrival myself. I was fairly certain it would be Nigel Hargreaves, since he was the only one who hadn't shown up yet. Sure enough, when I opened the door, a tall, gaunt-looking man stood there. He wore a raincoat and a tweed driving cap, his glasses were gold-rimmed, and his long, serious face brightened when he smiled at me.

"Do I have the pleasure of addressing Jennifer or Lucy?"

"I'm Jennifer," I said. "And I'm guessing you're Nigel Hargreaves."

He grimaced at that. "Is it because I'm the only gentleman?"

I laughed. "No. There are two of you. You are the last one to arrive, though."

"I'm very sorry. I'd hoped to be here earlier, but the traffic was difficult. I drove all the way down from the Lake District today."

The Lake District. That was where Anthea came from. I wondered if they lived close to each other. And would her carbon footprint be smaller if she had carpooled with Nigel Hargreaves? Or, since she'd taken public transportation, was it the same? I wasn't sure, but I was certain she'd calculate it. Maybe see if she could get a ride back with Nigel Hargreaves. I felt that more than worrying about her carbon footprint, Anthea worried about money. I could completely understand how difficult it was to run a small business. I was lucky that I was in a very special situation with free rent and a salary, so I didn't have to rely on the profits from The Scallop Shell, because they were still very slim. We were a brand-new business and building something from the ground up. Even though I'd come here on a three-month trial, I'd been hooked nearly from the start and determined to make a success of The Scallop Shell for a lot of reasons, partly to help Lucy, but also I had needed to create a new life for myself. And, all in all, I hadn't created a bad one.

I said that if he wanted tea, he should come right into the lounge where it was being served and I'd show him to his room later. He was perfectly happy to do that and walked in, not seeming at all fazed by the fact that he was walking into a room of chatting women and only one other man.

He smiled around the room broadly and said, "Good afternoon. I'm Nigel Hargreaves." And it seemed like he glanced around the room with affection. "I used to come to knitting retreats with my wife." He turned to me and said, "That's how I first began to knit. Joan never learned to drive, and after I retired, I used to drive her to the knitting shop and to knitting retreats, which she very much enjoyed. And one day I thought, why do I drive her to these places and then drive back home and spend a few days on my own? Why don't I learn to knit? And so I did. We used to sit together in the evenings watching television and knitting. It was very peaceful. Very companionable."

"When did you lose your wife?" Maggie Cooper asked him. No doubt she was getting ready to welcome him into the recently bereaved society that she and Beatrice had full membership in.

He shook his head sadly. "Joan hasn't passed away. She's in a home. She's forgotten she ever knew how to knit. Has no idea who I am." He seemed overwhelmed for a moment and looked at his shoes. And then he glanced back up again. "But when I come to a place like this and knit, I feel closer to her. I visit her in the home every day, but sometimes it's nice to escape for a few days. And, sadly, she won't notice that I'm not there."

Mrs. Biddle bustled in at that moment, having heard the new arrival, and said she'd be out with a fresh pot of tea. He sat down gratefully. Mrs. Biddle soon came out of the kitchen bringing him a plate of fresh shortbread along with the tea.

Rosalind said, "Your Joan, is she a tall woman who worked in finance, I believe it was?"

"Yes, that's right." He looked at the grandmother in surprise.

She nodded and said to Maggie, "You remember Joan. She was with us in Edinburgh and kept complaining about her memory going. She was a wonderful knitter, but we could see she was struggling with the pattern."

Maggie took in a quick breath. "Of course, I remember Joan. She's a lovely woman. I'm so sorry she's unwell."

Her husband seemed soothed that the two women remembered his wife, and he said how much she'd have loved coming to Cornwall to knit with us.

Anthea said she'd been there when we first came up with the idea of the knitting retreat, so we had to talk about having been at the marketing course in Oxford. This allowed her to segue into talking about her shop in the Lake District and how important it was to her that everything be locally sourced and organic. Then to my shock and probably Lucy's, she reached into her bag and pulled out small cloth bags tied with string, which makes them sound ugly, but they were actually nice, eco-chic, if you like. She passed one to every participant, explaining as she did so that the bags were filled with herbal tea for encouraging a good night's sleep. She smiled in her ingratiating way. "I know how difficult it is to sleep when you're not in your familiar home and bed. This is a little gift for each of you from me."

I smelled the lavender when she passed me mine and noted, unsurprised, that her card with all the details about her shop was attached. She'd done this in Oxford, too, given everyone a sample and a sales pitch for her shop. Lucy and I exchanged a glance. Trust Anthea to try to sell her wares the second she arrived.

"Isn't that lovely, dear," Maggie Cooper said, sniffing the bag delicately. "I'm sure the tea will be delicious. Very thoughtful."

Rosalind was squinting at the attached card. "And do you do hand creams as well? My hands get so dry with all this knitting."

"I do," Anthea said proudly. She pulled out a tube of the same hand cream she'd given Lucy and me when we'd first met. "I sell it on my website. You'll find all my products there."

Rosalind took the tube and said, "I won't try it just now as I'm knitting. And the ingredients are all natural, you say?"

"Organic and locally grown, yes. All from near my home in Keswick in the Lake District."

"Lovely," Sunita said. "My hands get dry too. May I try a little?"

As Rosalind passed her the cream, Anthea laughed and said to me, "Perhaps you should stock my hand cream in your shops, Jennifer and Lucy. In fact, I could design a cream specially for your shop."

I made a noncommittal noise, knowing I'd never stock her products. I didn't trust her enough.

There were murmurs of thanks from all the guests, and naturally, Anthea treated everyone to the story of how she sourced everything locally and it was all organic. She looked as virtuous as a saint, but I had my doubts that she was quite as eco-friendly as she pretended.

Lucy and I had planned this first afternoon as a session for everyone to get to know each other, and it worked well. Some knitted, Sunita brought her crochet out, and some of us simply chatted.

Rosalind was working industriously on her sweater, blue with red and yellow trucks in the pattern. "Is that for a grand-child?" Lily Tang asked her.

I could see there wasn't a question she could have been asked that would have pleased her more. "It's for my little Arthur. Four he'll be in July." Then she put down her knitting and pulled out her phone. "I have six grandchildren," she announced proudly. She passed the phone to Lily, who was either genuinely interested in a stranger's grandchildren or very polite.

"That's Arthur there," she said, pointing. I came around the back of the couch where they were sitting to see her family too. Six children were posing, each in a hand-knit sweater that I was fairly certain their grandmother had knit for them.

"And that's Susan, she's the oldest. She's twelve. Then Cameron, he's eight and such a poppet. And that's Rosie." Her voice wavered. "She's named after me." Rosie was obviously not well. She was sitting in a wheelchair, pale and thin. Along with a light cotton sweater in pink, she wore a knitted hat. "She had lovely red hair, she did. But it's gone now. Leukemia. She's nine and ever so brave." She took a shaky breath. "And that's Peter, he'll be five in January, and little April is my youngest grandbaby. She's six months old." April was held in the arms of Susan, and along with a pale pink cardigan, she sported a pink knitted dress, and there was a matching bow in her fair hair.

"They are beautiful children," Lily said. "No wonder you're so proud. And I very much hope your Rosie will be better soon."

"So do I. Such a time she's had, poor little mite. It started with eczema. She'd get these terrible rashes, and then she began to complain her tummy hurt. She lost weight and was just so listless, poor little soul. It breaks your heart. I'd take the disease from her in a minute if I could."

"Of course you would. You love them," Lily said in an understanding tone.

"There's nothing I wouldn't do for my grandchildren." She sighed. "At least I can knit and crochet. I've made Rosie some lovely soft animals. She's got a lion she loves, and I always tell her she's as brave as a lion."

Then she showed a few more photos of her grandchildren before putting away her phone and going back to her knitting. "What about you, Lily? Have you any children?"

"No. But I'm a proud auntie to my three nephews," she admitted, bringing out her own phone.

"I have three nephews as well," Maggie said, pausing in knitting her beret to glance up. "And two nieces. And one great-niece and one great-nephew. They are such a joy."

"I'm never having kids," Issy announced in a tone that was almost hostile. Wow, I thought, there's a story there. Then, as though she realized how she'd sounded, she added, "I mean, it's fine for some people, but I never want them."

"No," Anthea agreed. "The world's overpopulated as it is. That's why I chose to remain childless."

I could sense Rosalind getting ready to strongly disagree. Before there was a fight, I said, "I want to show you all the sweater I designed. Tomorrow, we're starting with a field trip to The Scallop Shell, the knitting shop that Lucy owns and I manage. You can pick up any supplies you need. You don't have to make the scallop shell sweater, obviously, but I will be teaching the scallop shell stitch for anyone who doesn't know it, and we'll have time to work on it together."

"Oh, that sounds nice," Sunita said. "Can I see your pattern?"

I pulled out the sketch I'd made and passed it around. "It's lovely," Lily said, and as she was so fashionable, I was thrilled with her approval. She tilted her head. "I might make it in several colors, rather than one."

"Yes," I agreed. "You could easily do that."

Beatrice took the sketch and commented on how lacy the pattern looked. "Lovely for a summer sweater, and I like the sleeve length. I shall definitely make this. Thank you, Jennifer."

Elliot thought he might be able to use the stitch in one of his designs.

"That's too complicated for me," Issy said, looking worried.

"Don't worry," Lucy reassured her. "We can work on a beginner project."

They'd be doing a simple scarf. As Lucy had confided to me, it was one design she was positive she wouldn't screw up. "Well," she'd amended. "Mostly positive."

CHAPTER 9

*B*ecause Tregrebi is not a large town, I had pre-booked dinners out. I'd sent out a list of the restaurants ahead of time, and while most of the retreat participants had signed up for all the dinners, Anthea had decided only to join us on the first and final meals. I hoped she didn't plan to cook in Mrs. Biddle's kitchen or there would be trouble. But now that I knew about her food issues, I wondered if she was more careful about restaurants than I would be. The Lucky Pearl was a Chinese restaurant that had plenty of room for a large group to dine as well as good food.

It turned out that Shadowbrook Manor boasted a passenger van that could seat seven people, so Mr. Biddle drove that and Lucy and I both drove our cars.

I liked The Lucky Pearl, with its red and gold decorations and tables that seated two to twenty.

As a group of ten, we were led to a large, round table. I'd phoned ahead to let them know we had a gluten-free vegan dining with us, and the waiter pointed out which dishes

Anthea could eat. She seemed quite happy with the extra attention, so I relaxed.

The dishes were placed on a lazy Susan in the middle, and we dined family-style, passing food or spinning the wheel and helping ourselves. A whole steamed fish that I hoped was local, its skin glossy with soy and ginger, was served alongside platters of Szechuan beef that crackled with fiery peppers, and kung pao chicken speckled with peanuts. There were tofu and simple vegetable dishes that Anthea could enjoy along with the rest of us.

Dessert was mango pudding and sesame balls.

Elliot had enjoyed a beer with his meal, but the rest of us had stuck to tea.

The restaurant was fairly full of locals and tourists, which I was happy to see, as I wanted the owners to be successful. I had met Rose Wong at an unofficial meeting of local retailers. She and her husband, Winston, had moved to Tregrebi from London and opened The Lucky Pearl.

While we were eating dessert, Rose Wong herself came out to greet us. She carried with her a basket of fortune cookies and passed them around. When she reached Lily Tang, Lily said something in Mandarin, and the two chatted briefly, laughing a couple of times. Then Rose wished us a very pleasant week and headed back to the kitchen.

"What were you speaking about in Chinese?" Anthea wanted to know.

Lily smiled. "We were laughing about the fortune cookies. They don't have them in China, you know. I think they began in America, but Rose says the tourists expect them even in Cornwall." She shrugged. "It's a fun and harmless way to end a meal." Then, as though to prove her point, she broke open her fortune and pulled out the slip of paper. "A chance meeting will lead to success and friendship," she read out. She glanced up, her dark eyes sparkling. "I certainly hope that this meeting will lead to successful knitting and new friendships," she said to us all.

A fresh pot of tea arrived then, and most of us put down our fortune cookies to refresh our tea.

Elliot went next with his fortune. "An unexpected relationship will become clear." For some reason he blushed and glanced at Issy.

Maggie broke open hers and read, "Embrace change. Don't battle it." She glanced at me. "Well, dear, if you plan to get me trying something different this week, apparently I must embrace it."

I didn't think the scallop shell sweater would challenge her very much, but if anything did, I'd remind her about her message this evening.

Then Beatrice broke open hers and started to read: "You will be—" Her anticipatory smile faded, and under her makeup, she paled. She scrunched up her paper. "Never mind. It's foolish nonsense." She reached for her tea, and I thought her hand trembled.

"You can't leave us in suspense," Elliot cried out. "You will be what? Rich and famous? Happy in love?" He reached for her discarded paper and, before Beatrice could stop him, read out loud: "You will be killed in a very painful way. You know what you did."

There was a terrible hush. No one seemed to know what to do, including me. I supposed this was my retreat and I'd better show some leadership. But what could I do?

"What kind of a fortune is that?" Elliot demanded, no

doubt feeling in some way responsible now that he'd broadcast the message.

"It's just nonsense," Beatrice reiterated. "Now let's move on. Agatha, it's your turn. What have you got?"

"I have a keen sense of humor and love a good time," she said flatly. "Everyone got one of those silly, hopeful messages. Why would you get something so dark?"

"Pass me that note," I said. Elliot, who was still holding it, passed Beatrice's fortune to me. I read the message in some wild hope that Beatrice and Elliot might have made an error and misread the message. They hadn't.

I looked at my own fortune and compared the two. I was no forensics expert, but it was pretty clear that the typeface was different. My message read, "Your talents will be recognized and suitably rewarded," in a font that didn't match the one in Beatrice's fortune. Even the paper seemed different. Everyone was watching me as I contemplated the two bits of paper. "Pass me your fortune cookie," I then asked Beatrice.

Beatrice passed over the two pieces, and I inspected them, again comparing hers with mine. It was impossible to tell, but her fortune cookie must have been tampered with.

"Do you think the company that makes them put the dark message in as a joke?" Rosalind asked.

I did not.

"It's not a very funny joke," Maggie said in a reproving tone.

I was thinking furiously. "Someone must have tampered with this." It was obvious, but I felt it needed to be said.

"Please, Jennifer, let's not make an issue of this. I promise you I shan't be looking over my shoulder," Beatrice assured me.

"Unless you have a guilty conscience," Anthea said and then tittered.

No one joined her, and she turned her inappropriate laugh into a cough and sipped her tea.

"If you'll excuse me, I think I'll go and freshen up," Beatrice said and disappeared in the direction of the ladies' room.

"I think the owners should be told and someone should report this to the company that makes the fortune cookies." Maggie had a point. "Maybe a former employee is angry with the owners of the restaurant and mixing in bad messages to scare away the clients."

Lucy said, "I think we should leave it for now. Beatrice is obviously wanting to forget about it."

I agreed, and as Beatrice headed back to our table, I started to talk about plans for the following day. Beatrice resumed her place and sipped tea as though nothing had happened. She'd put on some lipstick, I noticed, a bright red. The red lips looked garish on her pale face, like a bleeding wound, which was not an image I wanted in my head.

"Are you all right?" Rosalind asked, leaning over and patting her hand.

"Yes. Fine. But I won't be opening any fortune cookies for a while," she said with forced brightness. As though following her lead, the rest of the table agreed that her message had been in very poor taste. "I've a good mind to write to the fortune cookie company," Rosalind said. "I didn't like my fortune, either. Meet a handsome stranger? I'm a happily married woman. I don't like the suggestion."

We all laughed in relief at this moment of lightness.

Still, I couldn't shake the feeling that trouble was on its way.

When we arrived back at Shadowbrook Manor, I was so exhausted I just wanted to head back to our apartment and hang out with Lucy, but being the co-host of the retreat, I felt I had to be "on."

However, it was quickly apparent that everyone was tired. They'd traveled long distances, had work pressures, family pressures, and the strange occurrence at The Lucky Pearl hadn't helped.

Agatha said, "I'll be off now, if you don't mind, but I'll see you all bright and early for breakfast in the morning. Sleep well." And she was gone.

Rosalind stifled a yawn. "I think I'll go up now, too. Thank you for a lovely day."

Anthea said, "I'm going to brew myself my special tea so I sleep well. All of you should do the same. Good night."

And, one by one, they headed upstairs. I was so relieved.

Lucy and I headed to our apartment, and ignoring Anthea's tea, I made up a brew of my own that we chatted over until we were both yawning.

CHAPTER 10

$\mathcal{T}$he first day of the retreat went better than I could have imagined.

We started with breakfast, and Mrs. Biddle had outdone herself. Between the full Cornish breakfast, fresh fruit, toast, croissants, and coffee or tea, everyone was happy. Even Anthea, as one of the Biddles had clearly gone to the grocery store and bought some vegan, gluten-free cereal, coconut yogurt, and even a vegan, gluten-free bread with vegan butter to go on it.

Instead of eating in the breakfast room, we ate in the dining room so we were one big group. The weather was sunny, and maybe that helped contribute to the good mood that prevailed.

After breakfast, we went on a field trip to The Scallop Shell. I had sensibly decided that instead of creating a kit, I would show them the basic design and then we'd head to the knitting shop. Included in the price of their course was a certain amount of money towards whatever materials they wanted. Then if they wished to purchase anything else, they were welcome to, and we offered a ten percent discount.

Anthea only chose enough of a vegan yarn to use up her credit. Beatrice, on the other hand, bought two hard-cover knitting books and all the wools for a stylish coat designed by Teddy Lamont. "It's going to be a nice winter project while I'm sitting by the fire," she said. She also bought a very pretty pale green wool for her scallop shell sweater.

Sunita went for bold colors, and we would adapt the pattern for crochet.

Elliot had an idea that he could use the scallop shell stitch in a retro granddad sweater he was designing. I suggested to Nigel that he might want to work on something else, but he said he wanted to make the scallop shell sweater for his wife and wandered off to ask Maggie, who remembered his wife, for help choosing colors.

Since Issy was the only beginner, Lucy helped her choose a chunky wool that would knit up quickly into a scarf so she'd be less likely to give up in boredom. They chose a gorgeous cranberry color.

We returned in time for morning coffee, and all settled in to our projects.

Lucy taught the beginners, which was basically her and Issy sitting together chatting while they worked on the scarf. They were working in the library. When Lucy concentrated, she was a perfectly adequate knitter. It was just that I could see it wasn't something she was passionate about, so it was too easy to forget what she was doing, and then she'd drop stitches and mess up her tension, but she seemed perfectly focused with Issy. And while Issy clearly wasn't a proficient knitter, she caught on to the basics quick enough that soon they were working happily away.

I took the rest of the class, which wasn't as difficult as it could have been. Honestly, both Rosalind and Maggie were better knitters than I was. I was delighted to find that both of them loved my design, however. Still, I found, to my amusement, that a bit like those people online who comment on a great recipe and state all the ways they've changed it or come up with better ingredients, so the two best knitters took my basic idea and modified it to something that suited them better. Maggie immediately decided that she would lengthen the sleeves and alter the neckline, while Rosalind, not to be outdone by her knitting nemesis, decided that she would add a scallop shell frill to hers. I was keen to see how they both turned out.

I demonstrated the scallop shell stitch for those who didn't know it, and helped Sunita get started on the crochet version.

Elliot was a better knitter than I'd imagined, and when he told Rosalind that his gran had taught him to knit, she beamed at him and admitted that two of her grandsons liked to knit and so far, only one granddaughter.

Once we'd settled back in to knit, it didn't take long until my group was happily getting on with it, and then it became more like a knitting circle.

I was interested in why they'd all come, and naturally part of it was market research for me. If I was going to do more knitting retreats, what had appealed to them about this one? What had they come for? How did it differ from other retreats? Rosalind and Maggie pretty much went to as many as they could fit into their schedules around their other activities. They chatted about the various ones they'd been to. Maggie mentioned she'd always wanted to do a retreat on the Shetland Islands in Scotland.

Nigel said, "I went there with my wife." He sighed. "It was a lovely retreat." And then he looked a bit sad. "It was the last one my wife and I were able to do together."

Maggie looked sorrowful too. "I remember your wife very well. She was so clever. She and I could talk about everything from business to politics. She understood money and economics particularly well."

Nigel stopped knitting and looked at us. "The disease took her from me so slowly, I barely noticed."

"Such a very intelligent, accomplished woman," Maggie said. "I remember talking about the financial aspects of the European common market with her."

He nodded. "She was brilliant. And she was the one who always handled our family finances." He closed his eyes briefly for a moment. "I'm sorry to say I didn't realize how bad she was for a long time, or that she was making strange and rash investments."

"Oh, that's so sad." This was Beatrice. "How long was it until you found out?"

I thought that Nigel Hargreaves was one of those strong, silent types, and particularly one who had that classic British stiff upper lip where he didn't believe in sharing his troubles, but maybe there was something about sitting in a knitting circle with sympathetic women that made him open up, because he seemed almost to find relief in sharing his troubles with us. And it was an awful story. It turned out that his wife had been a brilliant and savvy investor, but her faculties deteriorated much more quickly than either of them had realized and she'd clearly begun making disastrous investments. He didn't share numbers, but it was pretty clear it had been devastating financially.

He said, "I don't mind for myself. I can sell the house and downsize anyway, but it meant I can't give her the best care available, and that's what hurts the most. I've moved her into a care home in Windermere, not too far from our home in Ambleside, but it's not the one I'd have chosen. I shall sell our home and find something small, closer to where she lives now."

I was shocked. "But isn't there some kind of remedy? If she was not of sound mind, couldn't those investments be refunded?"

He looked at me as though I was very naive, which was certainly true. He said, "If there had been proper paperwork, perhaps. But again, this wasn't at all like my wife, but she was making deals on handshakes with no paperwork, investing money in extremely shady enterprises. In fact, she was completely taken advantage of."

Anthea made a sound of annoyance as she dropped a stitch. "I must say I'm finding this pattern rather trying. I wonder if I'd do better in beginner's class with Lucy?"

I went over and sat beside her. It was true she wasn't as good a knitter as nearly everyone else in my knitting circle, but I felt she was a little more proficient than Issy, and after we went back a couple of rows, I was able to get her back on track. By that time, the conversation had moved on, and Rosalind was talking about her granddaughter Susan, who had won a prize at school in Latin.

"She's so clever. I'm going to knit her a special sweater

with a Latin saying. I can't remember it now, but it's something about getting better all the time."

"*Semper ad meliora*," Maggie said. "Always toward better things."

"Yes, that's it, Maggie. Thank you. Fancy you knowing Latin."

There was a pause. I was pretty sure that Maggie Cooper rolled her eyes, but she didn't say anything. She'd clearly been a clever child, too.

And then Beatrice said, "It's funny, I've been married four times. I never had children. When I was young, I didn't want them, but now that I'm older, I think how nice it would have been."

She'd been married four times? That seemed like a lot. I was too polite to say so, but Rosalind opened her eyes wide. "Four marriages. I guess I've been very lucky. My Walter and I have been married fifty years next year."

"That's something to be proud of, indeed," Beatrice agreed. "I've had such dreadful luck. A flying accident took my first husband, cancer robbed me of my second, my third was struck down by a tropical disease while we were visiting South America, and my last husband got the flu. That's all it was, flu. But it turned into pneumonia, and I was widowed yet again."

"That is tragic," Maggie said in sympathy.

And Rosalind added, "And there are no stepchildren?"

Beatrice pressed her lips together for a second, and for a moment I thought she might cry, but she didn't. She said, "My last husband had children, but I never met them. I don't think their mother approved of me."

That was all she said, but there was a world of story in

there, I could tell. She was an extremely attractive woman; had she lured a man away from his wife and family? And then I chided myself for being so judgmental. Maybe he'd already been a single man when he met her. But then why would his ex-wife have been so angry? It wasn't my business, but I was definitely curious. Who'd have believed we'd have so many dramatic stories within what seemed to be quite a placid knitting group?

"Well, I'm sorry you didn't have children because it means you won't have grandchildren," Rosalind said.

Nigel said, "It's clear you love your grandchildren very much."

Rosalind glanced up and smiled that lovely grandmotherly smile of hers. "They're my whole world. Much as I love my husband and my children, my grandchildren are the future, and they're so delightful and so very fond of me and I of them. I'd do anything for them. Cheerfully die. I've lived a good life, after all, and if anyone hurt one of my grandchildren, I would cheerfully kill."

There was a shocked moment, and Nigel said with a small smile, "Devotion indeed. No one can deny that the mother instinct is one of the primal forces in nature."

Before too long, Lucy and Issy appeared and said they were feeling left out. We made room for them in the big room and carried on. However, as the day progressed, I couldn't help but notice that while my group was diligently working away, Lucy and Issy seemed to be more engaged in conversation than knitting. I think it would be fair to say that their lips were doing a lot more moving than their knitting needles were. It wasn't my place to criticize, but I wondered if Lucy was even aware of it. It was one thing for Lucy to slack off during our knitting club meetings, but if Isabel was paying to learn how to knit, I felt she should be encouraged to do a little more actual knitting.

Sunita and Lily were close in age and both worked in finance, so they seemed to have bonded and chatted together as they worked. Maggie, Rosalind, and Nigel shared a couch and had become friendly, the two women seeming to have put their rivalry aside. At least for now.

Elliot sat beside Beatrice, talking about fashion. She, it turned out, had once modeled and went to as many high-end fashion shows as she could.

Agatha and Anthea sat together, though they weren't talking too much, and I moved from group to group, helping if I was needed or complimenting the color and design choices of those who didn't need my help. I tried to tell myself that the event was off to a good start, but I was aware of something beneath the surface, like a low hum only I could hear. It sounded like long-buried anger.

When Mrs. Biddle announced that afternoon tea was ready in the dining room, Lucy and Issy were quick to abandon their scarves. I wasn't sure how to handle it but really felt I should say something. I wondered if Lucy was even aware that she and her only student weren't sticking to the program. I told her I wanted to ask her opinion about something and took her into the library.

Lucy raised her eyebrows. "What's up?"

I didn't really know how to begin, so I said, "How do you think it's going so far?"

I couldn't have said anything more perfect, because before I even had to reference the fact that she and her student weren't knitting, she gave me a puzzled frown. "Honestly, I don't know why Issy's here. I really don't think she's interested in knitting. I mean, I know I'm not very good— I can teach the basics—but it's pretty clear she already knows how to do the basics and finds the whole thing as boring as I do. Why would someone who doesn't like knitting sign up for a knitting retreat?"

I asked, "Did she and Elliot know each other before this?"

Lucy wrinkled her nose. "I don't think so. They did arrive together, but he said that he'd seen her waiting at the bus stop and guessed that she was coming here."

"Is it true though?"

"I don't know. But why would they lie?"

"She just kept glancing in his direction. I can't figure out if she's got a crush or if they already know each other."

She wrapped her arms around herself, not giving herself a hug as much as protecting herself. "She seems kind of unhappy. Divorced parents, bitter mother, absentee father. Doesn't know what she wants to do in life. She's close to our age but seems a lot younger."

I nodded, pleased it was Isabel who was the head slacker and not Lucy. "Are you feeling some strange undercurrents in general?"

She glanced at me sharply. "I thought it was just me being hypersensitive. There's a strange energy in the air, and I feel like there's unspoken animosity."

"I feel that too. I mean obviously there's Rosalind and Maggie, who are clearly very jealous of each other and quite serious rivals, but they keep coming to the same retreats so they must be used to it."

"I know," Lucy agreed. "And Anthea's pushing her own products and doing her saintly routine. Nigel's obviously brokenhearted that his wife's not here. I just thought it would be more joyous, that's all."

I knew what she meant. "Do you think everyone's feeling it?" It was one thing for a couple of witches to be supersensitive to the atmosphere, especially when those witches were running their first retreat and very anxious for it to be a success, but if the people who'd paid money to come here were picking up on an uncomfortable atmosphere, they were not going to be inclined to tell all their friends about how wonderful it had been or in fact come again.

Again Lucy shook her head. "I just don't know."

"Well, hopefully when we start doing some more social things and getting to know each other better, the weirdness will disappear."

I really hoped that was true, though I had an awful foreboding that maybe it wouldn't be.

CHAPTER 11

$\mathcal{A}$fternoon tea was as incredible as it had been when Lucy and I had first sampled it. The scones were so good, even Agatha complimented Mrs. Biddle. Elliot ate so many sandwiches that Mrs. Biddle brought out a whole plate of them just for him, which made us all laugh. He had a cheeky way with her that she responded to. When he yawned hugely, she said, "Did you not sleep well last night? A young fellow like you?"

"To be honest, Mrs. B., I didn't. I'm afraid, Nigel, you snore."

Nigel looked very apologetic. "It's only when I sleep on my back. Perhaps you might try waking me and telling me to turn onto my side."

"Mate, I tried everything. You sleep like the dead. Only noisier."

"I took one of my sleeping tablets last night. Perhaps you'd like one tonight? They're very effective."

Mrs. Biddle said, "We can't have a healthy young man taking sleeping tablets." She shook her head. "All the rooms are full, but there is a pullout bed in the library. I'll make that up for you tonight. Ever so quiet it is in the library."

"That's very kind of you, Mrs. B.," Elliot said promptly, treating her to a grin that clearly melted her heart.

After she'd left, Issy leaned over and said, "Mr. Biddle wants to keep his eye on you, or you'll be stealing his wife from under his nose."

Issy was treated to an even warmer version of that smile. "I get on with women. Always have. It costs me nothing to be nice to her, and now I have a quiet place to sleep tonight." He glanced at his roommate. "No offense, Nigel."

"None taken. I'm only sorry to be such a poor roommate."

"You're not. Very tidy and considerate. You can't help snoring."

"I find a sleeping tablet helps me settle in a new place, too," Maggie Cooper said. "I even managed some warm milk, using the milk Mrs. Biddle so kindly left us for our tea, and adding hot water from the kettle. I slept wonderfully."

She and Nigel compared sleeping pill brands, and I zoned out. Until Anthea said, in that irritating way she had, "If you try my herbal tea, I think you'll find it gives you an excellent sleep without the strong medicine. Sleeping pills can be very addictive, you know."

One of those awkward pauses ensued until Sunita changed the subject by asking Anthea if her vegan afternoon tea was good.

Anthea looked like a saint about to be martyred. "The scones are rather dry, and the tofu spread in the sandwiches is rather tasteless, but I'm not one to complain."

Not much.

"At least you didn't get a threatening fortune cookie,"

Elliot said. I thought he was nettled that she was so ungrateful, especially as he and Mrs. Biddle seemed to be getting on so well, but it was an unfortunate comment as it brought up the whole sorry incident again.

"Gosh, I'd nearly forgotten that," Agatha said.

"I certainly have." No one could have been more bright and breezy than Beatrice Huntington-Cole.

Agatha continued, "Do you think the police should be called?"

Beatrice looked startled. "The police? Over a joke in poor taste? I wouldn't waste their time on such trivia."

Agatha chewed her bottom lip and then said, "Beatrice, you received a death threat."

Beatrice shook her head so hard, her diamond earrings danced around, catching the light. "How could a random fortune cookie be directed at me personally? And who would want to kill me?"

This was the tricky bit. "Are you sure you don't have any enemies?" I asked. Not that I agreed with Agatha exactly, but we should at least explore the possibility that someone had deliberately threatened Beatrice.

She seemed quite upset at the question. "I'm not a saint. Perhaps I sometimes rub people the wrong way. There's a woman on a charity committee I serve on who probably wouldn't be sorry if I never reappeared. Perhaps a man who was quite persistent in his attentions and whom I quite firmly turned down doesn't harbor the kindest of feelings towards me. But otherwise, I can't think of anyone."

I said, "But it's pretty clear that fortune cookie was tampered with. It didn't come out of the factory like the rest of them."

"Jennifer, dear, I completely understand you worrying, but please don't. Even if what you say is true, it couldn't possibly have been directed at me. I think we should all just put the unfortunate incident out of our minds and consider it as a tasteless joke." Then before I could even retort, she stood and said, "Is it too early for show and tell? I do love to see what everyone else is working on and how you interpreted Jennifer's beautiful design."

What could I do then? I felt like everyone was delighted to think about knitting and not that weird message. And maybe she was right, maybe somebody had thrown that in as a mean prank. It might not have been directed at her. As someone had said last night, it could have been an unhappy former employee, supplier or enemy of the Wongs trying to damage the reputation of the restaurant. Putting threatening messages in the fortune cookies was an excellent way to drive away business. I'd have a quiet word with the owners and let them know about the strange message. It could be the work of a disgruntled former staff member, or somebody who felt they'd had a bad meal, or who knew the kind of things that might cause someone to slip a frightening message into a random fortune cookie.

Still, even as Beatrice had urged me to throw the thing away, I knew I wouldn't. It was in a sealed bag in my bedroom, and there it would stay until I had a chance to show the Wongs.

Dinner that night was in a local pub famous for its fish and chips, and even though my senses were on high alert, there were no unfortunate incidents.

I went to bed that night and had trouble sleeping. Busby didn't help. I didn't think she liked being moved from our usual room and kept rolling around and waking me. The uneasy feelings I'd had all day, of swirling emotions that seemed quite dark, wouldn't leave me.

I tried to comfort myself with the thought that Lucy wasn't far away and settled down again to sleep. But when I finally did get to sleep, my dreams were about as restful as a wrestling match with a bunch of hungry alligators. I felt like I was pushing away things that were coming out of the dark to hurt me, and no sooner would they go under the surface than something else would rear up and bare its teeth at me. There were memories and fears that I'd tried to push down into my subconscious, and they would grab my ankle and bite down hard, usually when I was already stressed about something else and asleep. *He* kept rising in my dreams, the man who had nearly destroyed me.

In my dream I heard rain lashing against the window, as restless as the sea pounding the Cornish coast. It seemed to wake me, but somehow I knew I wasn't awake. In Boston, I'd left more than just a bustling city and a promising career; I'd escaped him—Vincent Blackwood, with his dark curls and darker arts, a sorcerer who'd woven magic and menace into my life until I fled. Cornwall was supposed to be my sanctuary, my fresh start far from his reach.

But tonight, he found a way back to me, through the pathways of my dreams.

I was walking through a fog-drenched forest, the mist thick and clinging, wrapping around my legs like cold fingers. The air tasted electric. I could feel him before I saw him—his presence, a familiar dread that crept up my spine.

"Jennifer." His voice was a whisper, yet it boomed through the silence of the woods, echoing off unseen trees.

I turned, and there he was, cloaked in shadow, his eyes glinting with evil. "You think distance can sever what binds us? I am as much in your soul as I am in these woods."

I backed away, but the forest closed in, the trees bending toward me, leaves whispering his incantations. "I left you, Vince. I left all of this," I said, my voice trembling as much as my hands.

He stepped closer, the ground beneath his feet frosted with a blue glow. "You can leave the city, but you can't escape from what you are, from what we are together. You belong to the world I showed you, the power you thirst for."

"I don't want it," I said. "I never wanted it." I'd believed he loved me, the man who financial newspapers called a stock market sorcerer. It was only later I discovered he'd started that moniker as a private joke. He was a practitioner of the dark arts, a sorcerer. The thing was, Vince had power and plenty of it. But for some reason he believed that together he and I could be unimaginably powerful. When he'd outlined our future as the ultimate power couple, my blood had run cold.

His laugh was low and haunting. "You may lie to yourself, but your power does not. It calls to me, even across the ocean." He reached out, and though I knew it was a dream, I felt his fingers brush against my cheek, seductive and frightening.

"Vince, please," I pleaded, the fog swallowing my words. "You don't need me. Leave me alone."

"You will return to me, Jennifer. By your will or mine." His voice hardened, and the chill that followed wasn't from the phantom breeze of the dream world.

I woke suddenly, my heart racing, and my cheeks felt the

ghost of his touch, chillingly real. I sat up in bed choking back my own cry. It had been as though he was there, his face was so clear. The worst thing was I had loved him once. And he had betrayed not only me but people I cared about.

I had taken myself away from everything I held dear to a new country and a new start. Even Lucy didn't know what had happened in Boston. I felt that she was safer not to know, especially now she had Rafe. And why would he come after me? I was far away now. But still, if I was ever going to go back to Boston in any kind of meaningful way, I was going to have to face up to what had happened, and maybe I would have to face him down, but I very much hoped that would never be my fate. I wrapped my fingers around the bracelet that Andrew had given me. It felt cold. Cold as death.

I got up and went into the kitchen to make some chamomile tea. Lucy's bedroom door remained closed, so hopefully she was sleeping peacefully. Once I had my tea, I walked out into the main room and looked out at the sea. Just for a moment, I was nearly certain I saw the masts of a ship that was no doubt being piloted by Gryffyn. I wondered if Dougan was out there surfing somewhere.

I crept past the library, not wanting to disturb Elliot.

I didn't feel ready to go to sleep. Some instinct caused me to walk upstairs. I didn't even know why, but I was wide awake, and I didn't have anything else to do. The stair treads were so solidly built that my steps were soundless. I got to the top, and all the doors were closed. Even from here I could hear snores that had to be Nigel Hargreaves. It was dark, and I don't know what I thought I was going to see, but clearly all was well up here. I turned to go back down when I was nearly certain I heard a door softly closing. I swung around, but in the dark, I couldn't tell which one it was. No doubt someone was coming back from the bathroom. Or even one of the people with en suite bathrooms could have shut the bathroom door and I'd somehow been able to hear it.

I crept forward, listening, but there was nothing. It seemed to me that the house slept, and it was time I did the same. I went back to my bedroom.

As I came down the stairs, I nearly jumped out of my skin as a ghostly figure came towards me. My hand went to my heart, and I could feel the amulet warming on my wrist. The ghostly apparition jumped and let out a squeak, and then I realized it was Issy.

"Isabel, what are you doing down here?" My voice came out more sharply than I'd intended, mostly because I was so alarmed and I had been about a nanosecond away from using my powers to throw her against the wall.

She looked as startled as I was. "I couldn't sleep," she said. "I was coming down to see if I could make some herbal tea or something. But then it was so dark in the kitchen, I didn't want to turn the lights on."

She was babbling, and it didn't sound remotely true to me. I was going to challenge her, and then it occurred to me it might not be herbal tea she'd been in search of so much as Elliot. What those two were getting up to was none of my business, and I felt the wisest course of action was to tell her I could make her a cup of herbal tea if she wanted it, but as I had suspected, she said no and that she was sleepy now and she'd head back to bed. I bade her sweet dreams and headed back to my own room, hoping very much that sweet dreams would also follow me.

I cannot say that they did.

Busby and I napped on and off sporadically for the remaining hours of the night, but when I awoke the next morning, I was not at my brightest or my best. Neither was Busby, but she simply curled up in the middle of the bed and went back to sleep. I had a knitting retreat to run.

Interestingly enough, when Lucy emerged from her room yawning, I could see there were dark circles under her eyes too.

"Blessed be," I said. She returned the greeting, and I said, "Did you sleep at all?"

She made a face. "Bad dreams."

I nodded. "Me too."

Then at the same moment, we both said, "Coffee."

We didn't have a full kitchen in the owner's quarters for the obvious reason that they'd had the huge kitchen, but there was a kettle and proper coffee and a small fridge that Mrs. Biddle had kept stocked for us as well as the other guests. I would have liked to think it was because she was kind, but I suspected she just wanted to keep me and Lucy out of her kitchen as much as possible.

I made the coffee while Lucy showered, and when she came out, she said, "Oh, bless you."

I was already half a cup down and took my turn in the shower.

She said, "What did you dream about?"

I couldn't tell her. I never had. I was closer to Lucy than anyone in the world, but I'd buried the trauma so deep I didn't want to unearth it. And besides, I felt like if I even talked to her about it, then I'd put her in danger. "I think I was just unnerved. I had those kind of vague dreams where you feel like something bad's coming but you don't know what it is."

She nodded. "Mine were something like that too. It's like there were, I don't know, monsters under the sea and they were trying to come up and get me. I didn't like it."

And I didn't like how eerily her dreams had mirrored mine. We were sisters bound not only by magic but also by a shared history, we'd been best friends for so long. I didn't like that maybe my trauma was infecting her in some way. I couldn't bear to think that I might put my best friend in danger. Though I wouldn't have come here if I'd thought that. I was pretty sure I was being completely fanciful and because I'd been thrown by the weird atmosphere yesterday and the fortune cookie incident, I was just too vulnerable to all the darkness I normally kept hidden.

I forced a bright smile onto my face and said, "Well, let's hope today is a better day than yesterday."

And how very much I wished that had turned out to be true.

CHAPTER 12

*E*veryone came down to breakfast on time except Anthea. Since Mrs. Biddle had gone to a lot of trouble to make her a vegan tofu scramble, she was less than pleased. However, everyone else seemed to go to extra lengths to make her feel appreciated, thanking her profusely for the truly delicious breakfast she laid out before us. I found that I didn't have much appetite. Still, I munched on some toast and ate some fruit salad.

I yawned and tried to cover it, but Maggie Cooper said, "You look tired, Jennifer. Bad sleep?"

"Just a bad dream," I assured her.

"I had the most dreadful sleep last night. I seem to have mislaid my sleeping tablets." She looked somewhat accusingly towards Nigel Hargreaves. "Nigel, I know we discussed sleeping pills, but you wouldn't have taken my sleeping pills, would you?"

He looked horrified at the idea. "Of course, I wouldn't. I would never go into your room uninvited." Then realizing what he'd said, he blushed hotly. "What I mean is, I would never go into your room at all. Besides, I have my own sleeping pills. Although, now you bring it up, I couldn't find mine last night, either."

He looked at his young roommate. "I don't suppose you—"

"No, I didn't take your sleeping pills. I'm twenty-seven. I don't need sleeping pills. Earplugs. That's what I need when you start snoring, mate. But the pullout in the library was quite comfortable. I slept well." He shot a cheeky glance at Issy, who dipped her head toward her plate so her hair fell forward, covering her cheeks, but not before I'd seen the secret smile.

Mrs. Biddle was in and out, but after about ten more minutes, she clucked and said, "I suppose I'd better take that vegan scramble into the kitchen and set it to warm."

I took the hint. "I'm sure Anthea's just slept in. I'll go and see if she's awake."

I really wasn't sure that this was the best idea. If somebody had joined a knitting retreat and wanted to sleep in for a morning, shouldn't we let them? Especially if that someone was Anthea, who had a nasty habit of setting people's backs up. She was so relentlessly virtue signalling that you couldn't help but feeling guilty for a lot of your choices. It was like trying to hang out with a saint. Although I liked to think that most saints would have been more tolerant of people who were less perfect than themselves.

I rose from my chair and excused myself. Lucy looked up. "Do you want me to go?"

I would have vastly preferred anyone to go up there but me. I didn't want to barge in on Anthea Fitzgerald's beauty sleep. But I felt like, as I was the one who had wanted to host this retreat, I should take responsibility for rousing the late-comers, so I said, "Don't worry about it. I'll just peek in. If she's sound asleep, I'm not going to wake her up. She can catch up on her knitting later."

Elliot glanced up at me and with a quick glance towards the closed kitchen door said, "And her vegan scramble."

There was a rumble of amusement around the table, and I left them chuckling. At least everyone seemed to be in a good mood this morning, including Beatrice, who looked, unlike me and Lucy, like she'd slept beautifully. Her makeup was perfect, her hair unmussed, and her outfit effortlessly country casual. If Jodie Rymer and the Cornwall Today! team showed up and wanted to do a feature about the knitting retreat, Beatrice Huntington-Cole was camera-ready.

I ran up the stairs and knocked softly on Anthea's door. There was no answer. No doubt she was sleeping. Still, I thought she might be the kind of person who would complain if she hadn't been roused and she missed so much as five minutes of the course she had paid for. It was probably that thought that caused me to open the door. I did so care-fully. It wasn't locked.

I don't know what hit me first. A sense of dread? The odd smell? Something did. The curtains were drawn, and the room was dark, and there was a cowardly part of me that just wanted to back away and close the door again, but I couldn't. I stepped forward.

"Anthea?" I called softly. There was no answer. In truth, I hadn't expected there to be. I could feel that my hand was shaking as I hit the light switch. If I'd thought more clearly, I'd have probably crept forward and opened the curtains a little just to illuminate the area, but I didn't want to take a step into that room, not with the dark energy that was in there. The room sprang to light immediately when the overhead light came on.

She was lying face down on her bed.

"Oh no," I heard myself moan, and then my back hit the wall, mostly to prevent myself from sinking to the ground in a trembling heap.

To my enormous relief, Lucy appeared behind me. She said, "I felt that you needed me." Then her gaze took in what mine had already seen. "Oh, no," she moaned.

Anthea wore a white linen nightgown, but there was no possible way she was asleep. A knitting needle protruded from her back like a dagger.

Lucy said in a high, unnatural voice, "She was stabbed in the back with a knitting needle?" It was so ridiculous, I felt a bubble of laughter trying to climb up my throat. I swallowed it down hard.

I looked at her. "That couldn't be enough to kill a person, surely?"

She said, "We should make sure. Maybe she's alive."

But we both knew she wasn't. Her spirit was gone. There was nothing left but the darkness of an unnatural death. Still, the police would ask us, and we'd sound both cowardly and uncaring if we said we hadn't even checked to see if she was alive or dead.

"I'll do it," I said. I trod gingerly forward and picked up her wrist to check for a pulse. It was no surprise to me that there wasn't one. Her body was cold. I glanced around rapidly. There was no sign of struggle that I could see with my untrained eye. An empty mug sat on the nightstand, her bag of herbal tea open beside it. Her glasses were folded neatly atop a folded newspaper. She'd been doing the crossword puzzle and hadn't finished it. Somehow that struck me with deep sadness. She'd gone to bed wondering about an eleven-letter word for crafty deception and died before the answer came to her.

"Lucy? Jennifer?" Maggie Cooper's voice came up the stairs. "Is everything all right?"

Quickly we exited the room and shut the door behind us. "Just stay downstairs," I yelled back. I had my phone in my pocket and made the call to 999.

CHAPTER 13

*W*aiting for the police to arrive was torture. Lucy and I had held a hurried conference in the hallway before we'd headed back downstairs. We agreed that we couldn't say anything to anyone about what had happened to Anthea, particularly not details such as the knitting needle sticking out of her back.

When we came back down to the breakfast table, everyone stopped eating and drinking and turned to look at us. It was as though our terrible news went before us. And one look at our faces must have confirmed that something bad had happened.

It was Maggie Cooper again who said, "For heaven's sake, what's wrong? The pair of you look like you've seen a ghost."

I stuck to the script that Lucy and I had frantically agreed on. "I've called an ambulance, but I think they might be too late. Anthea's cold and she's not breathing."

There were sounds of shock and horror around the table. Maggie said, "But I must go up to her. I learned CPR years ago. I think it's three breaths in and...no, wait a minute, one breath in and so many chest presses. Oh dear." She put a hand to her head.

Then Elliot stood up. "I had to take CPR for a mountaineering course. I'll go."

He came towards us, and I put a hand up. "There's nothing you can do, Elliot. She's definitely dead."

He jerked back as though the hand I'd placed against his chest was an electric fence. He looked at me, and I could imagine him in charge of a team of mountaineers on a tricky climb. "Are you absolutely sure?"

"I am. There can be no doubt. I think she died sometime in the night."

He nodded and went back to his seat and sat down. He picked up his cup of coffee, put it back down, reached for water and drained his water glass. No one knew what to say.

Rosalind said, "I can't believe it. A heart attack, do you think?" She turned to Maggie, and for once, the two rivals seemed like friends who could rely on each other.

Maggie made a face of disbelief. "But she was so young. And so healthy. That vegan diet. Everything so pure."

Gravely, Nigel Hargreaves said, "I'm not quite sure that's true." Every eye turned to stare at him. He colored slightly under the gray tinge of his skin. "I'm not one to speak ill of the dead, but I can tell you for a fact that many of her claims were untrue."

"Pardon?" Sunita said.

"I'm a keen gardener, you see, and from the Lake District myself. I can tell you that she couldn't possibly be growing all the plants and herbs she claims to be growing in the Lake District. The climate simply won't support it."

Issy said, "But couldn't there be like, I don't know, a microclimate? I mean, my mother grows roses in an enclosed spot beside stone walls, which she calls a sun trap."

He looked a little sheepish. "I've studied her supposed farm. It's not a sun trap." He thinned his mouth and didn't say any more. Everybody else might be surprised, but certainly Lucy and I weren't. His opinion concurred exactly with that of Margaret Twigg, who had said she was a fake.

In fact, Sunita voiced that very thought. "Are you saying she was a fake?"

He shrugged his shoulders. "I think if you analyze that tube of cream she gave you, you will discover it isn't hand-made in small batches in the Lake District. I suspect she buys it cheap from a thoroughly unsavory factory and repackages it."

I felt my eyes narrowing. He'd clearly put a lot of thought and research into this. For a woman he'd just met two days ago? Why?

Mrs. Biddle emerged from the kitchen, obviously ready to clear up after breakfast, and found everyone sitting there in various stages of shock. She sent a puzzled glance first to Anthea's obviously untouched spot and then looked around at the rest of us.

"Whatever's happened?" Before I could speak, she said, "Is the young lady ill?"

If only it was that. This time Lucy spoke up, for which I was very grateful. She said the same thing I had already told the bigger group, that we had found Anthea cold and unre-sponsive, clearly dead, and that the ambulance and police were on their way.

Mrs. Biddle held on to the table for a moment for support

and then said, clearly to herself, "And there I was raining curses on her head in the kitchen. Oh, poor lady." And then she said, "I've always said it's not healthy to eat nothing but plants." And then she turned around and walked back into the kitchen. I was certain it was only stress that had made her say that, but it hadn't been the most sympathetic thing I'd ever heard.

Finally, Elliot, who clearly had leadership qualities, said, "Are we just going to sit here and wait for the police?"

Issy looked at him. "What else do you suggest we do?"

"I think we should go back to the lounge and knit. At least it would give us something to do until the emergency services arrive."

It was an excellent idea. I should have thought of that. I tried to pull myself together. In fairness, Elliot hadn't been the one to find Anthea and so couldn't know that she'd been horribly murdered. Still, his common sense snapped me back, and I led the way. Like kids at school, we all settled in the same seats we'd sat in the day before. The chair where Anthea had sat remained conspicuously vacant. I couldn't teach anything and pretty obviously Lucy couldn't either, and I didn't think it would have been appropriate. We all just picked up our knitting or crochet and carried on. There was absolutely no conversation, so it seemed shockingly loud when Mrs. Biddle came in with a tray of tea and her famous shortbread biscuits.

She said, "I've brought you tea. They say it's good for shock."

I wouldn't have thought I could have stomached tea, but surprisingly it was a welcome gesture. Every one of us put down our knitting and got up to make tea.

"Put plenty of sugar in it, mind. That's good for shock," she said and then disappeared back into her quarters.

I'd barely taken a sip of my tea when the front doorbell rang. I jumped up, and Lucy came with me. When we got to the front door, two paramedics stood there.

I led them upstairs. They went up swiftly, but it didn't take them long to confirm what I'd discovered. There was absolutely no possibility that Anthea Fitzgerald was going to be revived. It wasn't long after that the police arrived and right behind them, two detectives. They both showed their ID, but I already knew one of them. Sergeant Frances Draycott was about my age, and she obviously recognized me, too, for she gave me a brief nod. The older man with her introduced himself as Detective Inspector Tom Barnsley. He looked like a family man who could as easily have sold insurance or worked in a bank as become a detective. His hair was salt-and-pepper and thinning, his voice soft when he introduced himself and his sergeant. This time Lucy and I went up together with the two investigators.

They put on those disposable bootie things and went in while Lucy and I stood outside in the hallway, waiting. After a few minutes, DI Barnsley came out.

"Who found her?"

"I did," I said.

"What time was this?"

Because I'd glanced at my watch before I went upstairs, I knew exactly what time it had been. "Nine forty-five?"

"And did you touch her?"

I shuddered at the feel of her cold flesh under my fingers. I swallowed. Nodded. "I picked up her wrist to see if I could detect a pulse."

"And could you?"

I knew he had to ask these questions, but it was brutal to hear them aimed at me in that brisk way. I shook my head. "She was cold. No pulse."

"When did you last see her alive?" I told him last night, and then I explained that we were having a knitting retreat. "Is everyone else accounted for?"

"Yes. We were all having breakfast when I went to check on her, as she hadn't come down."

He glanced up and down the corridor. "Who else has access to this house?"

I shrugged helplessly. "The exterior doors were locked. I really don't think anyone came in. And her bedroom's quite high."

He nodded. "No doubt you're right, but we have to check all these things."

I told him I honestly didn't know. I didn't think the locks had been changed after the last caretakers had left, but Rafe would know that better than I would. Could former guests have gone away with keys? Were there tradesmen who had keys? I didn't know. I suggested that Mrs. Biddle might be the best person to ask about that.

He looked thoughtful. "What did you tell them downstairs?"

I was mildly proud of Lucy and me for having the sense to keep certain details to ourselves. I told him exactly what we'd told them, that we'd found her dead and that was all.

He nodded. If he approved, there was no sign of it. "You didn't tell them about the knitting needle stabbed into her back?"

I flinched at the words, as though I would feel a knitting needle pushing its way into my own back. "No. We didn't."

Then Lucy said, as though she couldn't prevent herself, "But could a knitting needle really kill a healthy person?"

He looked at her sharply. "I wouldn't have thought so. There's quite a lot of investigation yet to be done. I am pleased you two had the sense not to spread all the details of what you found. I hope you'll continue to do so."

We both nodded, and then he came downstairs with us. I heard light steps running down, and Sergeant Draycott joined us.

The group was attempting to knit, but it didn't look very heartfelt. It was as though people just wanted something to do with their hands and hopefully a way to occupy their thoughts.

Soon the forensics team arrived, and the upstairs took on a life of its own.

Then Maggie Cooper said, "I'm very sorry, Jennifer, but I really don't think I'm comfortable staying here any longer. I want to go home."

"Yes, so do I," Sunita agreed immediately.

The chief inspector shook his head. "I'm afraid I must ask you all to remain where you are. This is a murder investigation."

Maggie Cooper dropped her knitting. "Murder? Did you say murder?"

"I did. Anthea Fitzgerald was murdered. And, as each of you is a witness, I must ask you to remain where you are."

Sunita looked bewildered. "But I came here for relaxation. This is not doing my stress levels any good at all. Anyway, if she was murdered, who murdered her?"

"That's what we hope to find out," he said.

"But if there's a murderer in Tregrebi, I am very sorry, but I do not feel safe."

I felt like telling her it wasn't just Tregrebi she had to worry about; it was this very house.

"I'll station a police officer here. You'll be quite safe."

Elliot glanced around. In a calm tone, he said, "There's no sign anyone came into the house last night. I think what you're saying, sir, is that the murderer must be one of us."

CHAPTER 14

*T*o say that Anthea's murder put a damper on our knitting retreat would be the grossest of understatements. And yet we were stuck with each other in Shadowbrook Manor, and since we weren't allowed to leave, what could we do but knit? Frankly, I'd never been so pleased to be a knitter, because even as my mind was working furiously, trying to work out what had happened, when it had happened, how it had happened, and who had done it, I could at least keep my hands occupied, and that seemed to help.

I wasn't sure what everyone else was thinking, though I was fairly certain that Lucy's thoughts were going along the same path as mine were, but it seemed like all of us dug into our knitting with relief. Even Issy, who wasn't the most diligent of students. And one by one, the police took us into the dining room, which had been set up as command central, and interviewed us.

The forensics team spent ages upstairs, and probably the worst moment since the one where I had discovered her body was when they carried the stretcher, with the remains of Anthea, out of the front door.

We all came out to the foyer and watched as she was taken out. No one had asked us to, obviously, but also no one stopped us. It was a little like a funeral procession. We were all quiet and solemn. Rosalind had her head bowed, and her lips were moving. I suspected she was praying.

After the stretcher was placed into an ambulance and the door shut, Nigel raised his head and made the sign of the cross. I was so surprised, I blurted out, "You're Catholic?"

He smiled. "Not a regularly practicing one, but I do find the rituals are soothing in times of distress."

Maybe that was sort of what we were doing with our knitting, too. It was a soothing pastime for all of us.

Even though I'd been briefly interrogated when the police first arrived, I was the first one called into the dining room to be interviewed. I felt horribly nervous and uncomfortable but also kind of happy to be the first one in here so that I could get it over with. The two detectives were in there, there was a laptop, and they asked me the same questions again. When I had last seen Anthea, which had been the night before when she'd gone to bed, and when and how I'd found her.

Then the lead detective just looked at me and said, "And the victim signed up to come to a knitting retreat?"

I didn't like the way he said that, as though knitting retreat was code for something else. What did he think we were doing?

My tone came out slightly sharp as I said, "Yes. That's right. A knitting retreat."

He nodded as though letting me know I could tone it

down a bit. "Did you know Ms. Fitzgerald before you met at this knitting retreat?"

"Yes. I did." And then I explained how Lucy and I had both met Anthea at a marketing course for independent retailers in Oxford, and in fact that was where I had first come up with what I now considered a terrible idea to run a knitting retreat. I felt myself going back in memory to being in Oxford and talking about the retreat. "Anthea was very supportive of the idea, even in Oxford, and at that moment said she'd be interested." I hoped the distaste I had felt for the woman didn't come through in my voice, but since he was a detective he could probably hear it. "I didn't even know she could knit. But sure enough, when we started putting out the word that we were running our very first knitting retreat, she signed up quite early on."

He wasn't taking notes. He was letting the other detective do that. He just looked at me, my face, and probably my hands, which made me self-conscious about the way I could feel my two hands holding on to each other as though giving each other comfort. I tried to relax. I hadn't done anything wrong. I didn't know why he was making me feel like I was guilty of something.

He said, "Did you specifically let Ms. Fitzgerald know you were running this retreat?"

I shook my head and then said, "No."

He seemed to ponder that. "I would have thought, since she'd said she was interested in the course, that you might have emailed her or messaged her to let her know it was on. You must have been anxious to get enough people since it was your first one."

If I'd been a detective, I would have asked that very question. He wasn't saying, did you like the woman? Did you have any reason to murder her? But he was certainly getting to my feelings about the dead woman. Because obviously, if it had been someone I'd really liked, I would have been keen to invite them to the first retreat. I tried to keep my voice neutral.

"I'm not sure I thought she was really serious about coming to the retreat. And I think Lucy and I both wanted to give the opportunity to our regular customers first."

"How did you advertise the knitting retreat?"

I thought about it. "We sent out newsletters to our customer base and our newsletter list. I put a sign in my window. Lucy may have done the same; you'll have to ask her. And then we used social media, Instagram, Facebook."

He nodded. "Who else knew that Anthea Fitzgerald was coming here?"

"I think quite a few of them mentioned that they were coming to the retreat in their own social media." I had to be honest with him. "I had encouraged everyone to do that. We had some sharing buttons embedded within the newsletter." I looked up at him helplessly. "It's something they suggested in the marketing course we took."

He nodded. No doubt somebody would be trolling through all the Instagram feeds.

"Did she have any enemies?"

I shrugged helplessly. "I really barely knew the woman."

"Would you have guessed, for instance, that she was in financial trouble?"

He couldn't possibly know so much about Anthea already, could he? I wondered if he was just fishing. Or maybe they'd found something in her room. I thought about it. "I can't say I'm surprised if that's true. I didn't know for sure, but I remember in Oxford her credit card got declined, but then that can happen for all kinds of reasons. And when we did a field trip to The Scallop Shell, our knitting store here in Tregrebi, she kept to the budget." Then I had to explain that I had included a certain amount of credit for buying whatever wools and supplies people wanted to, and then anything above that they had to buy on their own. I said, "Most people spent more than what had been budgeted, but I noticed that Anthea was very careful to stay within the budget."

"Mmm."

"She could simply have been frugal," I reminded him.

He just nodded. "Your knitting retreat had only been going, what? A day?"

I closed my eyes briefly. "Yes. This was day two of the retreat, though everyone arrived a day before that."

"Did it seem to you that she had any enemies among the other participants? Was there any animosity you spotted?"

I thought about Mrs. Biddle and the vegan/gluten-free announcement that Anthea hadn't bothered to put on her intake form. And why hadn't she? It was such a simple thing to do. But she'd caused a lot of trouble by neglecting to do so. I tried to put into words my feelings about Anthea Fitzgerald.

"She could be a difficult person. She was very proud of the fact that her products were organic and vegan and all grown locally. She only wore natural fibers, took public transit for her carbon footprint, was vegan and gluten-free and maybe a little bit saintly about it all. Like she was better than anyone who made different choices. I think it could get people's backs up."

"Speaking of backs, it was a curious way to find someone dead. A knitting needle in the back. Can you think of any reason why someone would do that?"

I shuddered. It was a full-body shudder from the top of my scalp to the soles of my feet. I felt like I was back in that room again, smelling that smell and feeling the horrible darkness of death. It took me a second just to take a breath. Then I said, "Maybe that was the weapon that was closest?"

"The killer would have had to be extraordinarily strong and extraordinarily lucky in subduing the woman long enough to hold her still and poise the knitting needle in a spot that would penetrate her ribs and hit the heart. And they'd have to keep her quiet while they were doing it."

I felt confused. "What are you saying? That it was more than one person working together?"

"We've barely begun the investigation, but I think you could see for yourself that there clearly hadn't been much of a struggle."

"Did they come at her while she was asleep?"

"Or she was already dead. And the knitting needle was inserted postmortem."

"What?!" The question burst out of me. "Someone killed her and then shoved a knitting needle in her back? Who would do such a thing?"

He didn't exactly smile, but his eyes lightened briefly. "That's what we're here to find out."

I was so stunned, I just sat there for a minute. "You mean like they smothered her with a pillow or something?"

He seemed to be debating and then said, "Do you know if Ms. Fitzgerald was in the habit of taking sleeping pills?"

I shook my head. "I really don't. But she was so careful

about what she put into her body, I would have been surprised. She brought us all samples of a special blend of tea she said would help us sleep. She said she was going to make herself a drink in her room when she went to bed. I don't know for sure that she didn't take sleeping pills, but I'd be surprised."

"How about you? Do you take sleeping pills?"

He'd asked so suddenly, I felt startled by the question. "Never. I generally sleep quite well, and if I don't, I catch up on my sleep the next night, I guess."

"Did anyone at your knitting retreat use sleeping pills that you know of?"

It's funny how a conversation comes back to you that you didn't know you'd remembered. It wasn't until he asked me if anyone was taking sleeping pills that I suddenly remembered the conversation between Nigel Hargreaves and Maggie Cooper.

I said, "Two of the retreat guests talked about how difficult it is for them to get to sleep on the first night in a new bed. It was Maggie Cooper and Nigel Hargreaves. Maggie confided to Nigel that a cup of warm milk and a sleeping pill sorted her right out. She even offered him one of her sleeping pills, but he said he wouldn't trouble her; he had his own."

"So that's two of your guests you can confirm had sleeping pills with them."

"I can confirm that's a conversation I overheard." I hadn't actually seen anyone take a sleeping pill. "This morning they both said they couldn't find their sleeping pills last night."

He nodded and I saw Detective Draycott scribble down a note. "Was Ms. Fitzgerald's room locked this morning?"

"No."

"Were you surprised?"

I really hadn't been. "Four of the rooms, including Anthea's, weren't en suite, so they needed to use the bathrooms in the night. And, I don't know, it was such a friendly group. I'd be surprised if anyone bothered to lock their room. The front door was certainly locked at night."

He had asked me for a plan of the bedrooms and who was sleeping where. Rather than do anything complicated, I took a letter-size piece of paper from the notebook in my bag, turned it so it was rectangular, and drew two lines in the middle to represent the corridor, with steps leading up at one end and two full bathrooms at the other. Then I drew eight boxes, one for each room.

I began with Room 1, on the ocean side, and wrote Beatrice Huntington-Cole (en suite). Next to her in Room Number 2 was Maggie Cooper (en suite). Beside Maggie was Lily Tang in Room 3 (shared bathroom), then on the end closest to the two bathrooms was Anthea Fitzgerald in Room 4 (shared bathroom). Across the hall from Anthea's room was Room 5, occupied by Issy Sterling (shared bathroom); beside her was Sunita Rai, in Room 6 (shared bathroom); then in Room 7 was Rosalind Wallace (en suite); and finally, across the hall from Room 1 and by the stairs, was Room 8, occupied by Nigel and Elliot, also en suite. Then I made a note that after suffering Nigel's bad snoring his first night with us, Elliot had moved down to the library on the main level and slept in a sofa bed.

I passed the rough sketch to DI Barnsley, who studied it for a moment.

"So, the four rooms nearest the two bathrooms would likely have people coming and going and leaving their rooms unlocked. However, you say no one locked their doors, so anyone could have accessed Anthea Fitzgerald's room last night."

"Yes, I suppose so." I glanced at the sketch I'd drawn. Pictured nefarious figures sneaking down the corridor to do Anthea harm.

Skulduggery. That was the eleven-letter word she'd been looking for. There'd been some serious skulduggery going on last night at Shadowbrook Manor.

"Thank you, Ms. Cunningham. This is very helpful. Can you remember anything at all from last night that you haven't yet told us?"

I liked the open-ended question. It made me open my mind and try to catch any actions or overheard conversation, anything I might have noticed and not registered at the time.

I remembered feeling restless and going upstairs in the middle of the night, around two a.m., to check that everything was okay. I'd heard a door close. I related the experience to the detectives, not even certain if it was relevant, but I figured the more information they had, the better, and if it wasn't useful, they could discount it. I had a feeling that in investigating a crime, the detectives never knew what was going to be useful and what wasn't. Had someone just gone to the bathroom in the middle of the night, or had I actually heard the murderer entering or leaving Anthea's room? And even as I tried to pinpoint where I had actually heard the sound and exactly what it had sounded like, I could come up with nothing more than hearing the click of a door shutting. I did not think it had been a bathroom door inside someone's room simply because the sound insulation was better than that, but I couldn't be certain.

"Thank you. I may call on you again, but for now, could you send Lily Tang in?" She was the person who'd had the room beside Anthea's. Did he think she'd heard something? Of course, she'd also been the closest to that room if she had murder on her mind.

At the end of the day, we all had more knitting accomplished than we'd had in the morning, but I didn't think any of us had particularly enjoyed the activity. At one point, Issy tossed down her work and said, "I hate knitting." Whereupon Lucy had been extremely sympathetic and said, "I know. I've often felt that way. But if you persevere, it does get easier."

I wasn't certain who she was trying to convince.

At three, Mrs. Biddle brought in the tea, and it almost made me sad not to see the vegan scones and the oat cream that she'd had to substitute for the clotted cream the rest of us had. We had been scheduled to go out for another meal, but a quick discussion confirmed that none of us felt up to it, so I was able to get pizzas delivered.

We were a somber group gathered in the dining room eating pizza.

Elliot glanced at Issy while they were eating dinner and said, "Fancy going out to the pub this evening?"

She glanced at me. "Are we allowed?" I had no idea whether we could go out, given that we were all suspects in a murder investigation.

But Elliot snapped, "Unless the police are prepared to arrest me, I won't be stuck in this house as though I'm in prison. What do they think we're going to do, murder the villagers?"

"Elliot!" Maggie scolded him. "This isn't the time to be facetious."

I said, "Let me check with the officer on duty." Because they had left us one, a young guy in uniform, and that was altogether unnerving. I knew how the others felt, but I didn't actually feel safer with a cop in residence. It was just a constant reminder, if we needed one, that a terrible crime had been committed here. And probably by one of us.

The officer asked where the pub was and what time they thought they'd be home, and must have checked in because the answer was yes. Elliot, who looked like he'd been spoiling for a fight if anyone had tried to stop him, nodded briskly. Then he glanced around at the rest of us. "Anybody else fancy going to the pub?"

To be honest, I was strongly tempted. Shadowbrook Manor was starting to feel like a prison. But in the first place, I thought Elliot was more interested in romancing Issy than chatting to the rest of us, and second, I felt like I needed to stay here, so I declined the treat, as did everyone else.

Then Nigel Hargreaves suddenly said, "Actually, I think I would like to go and have a pint. Not to be festive, just to get away for a bit, stretch my legs. Rosalind? Maggie? Sunita?"

Maggie fluttered her hands. "Oh, well, I don't know. I don't usually—"

"Come on. It'll do you good. You don't have to drink alcohol. You can have a cup of tea if you want. Just be good to get out and see some other people."

Maggie glanced at Rosalind and then at Sunita, who was the first one to say yes. And then the others agreed to go along as well. My feeling was that as long as they stayed together, there was safety in numbers.

So in the end, there was only me and Lucy left. She let out a sigh of relief when they left, all turning down the offer of a lift. Every one of them agreed they wanted to stretch their legs and walk into town.

As they were leaving, I said, "Make sure you stay together. Or at least in pairs." I just had this horrible vision of something bad happening if one of them somehow got separated from the others.

Sunita widened her eyes in alarm and then nodded briskly. The thing was, they all seemed so nice.

How could one of my lovely knitters have killed another one? It was inconceivable.

CHAPTER 15

*A*fter they had left, Lucy brewed us a clarifying tea, and we sat together. We'd barely begun commiserating with each other when a deep voice said, "I hear there's been a spot of bother."

I jumped out of my skin and turned to see Gryffyn Penrose standing in the shadows, near an alcove that curved away from the veranda doors.

"Gryff, don't you ever use the front door?" I scolded him because he'd startled me so.

He shook his head slowly. "As rarely as I can manage. And as I've seen you've had the law hanging about, I've been in no hurry to announce my presence."

I could believe there'd been a price on his head in the last three hundred years, and I understood he was cautious about interacting with day walkers, as he called us, and respected that. I supposed authorities of any kind could lead to awkward questions, and the last thing he wanted was anyone investigating him too deeply. Rafe had worked diligently to make sure he passed as currently human, but I had a feeling

Gryff cared much less about fitting in with society. He'd been a renegade back in the day, and time had not changed him.

I said, "It's more than a spot of bother when someone comes here for a knitting retreat and ends up dead."

"Murdered, I hear," he clarified.

I nodded.

"I heard a rather garbled account," he said. "Mr. Biddle told Robin Trebilcock, who passed it on. I feel that some things got missed in the translation. It was rumored that a woman was murdered with a knitting needle. That can't be possible."

"That's what I said," I cried out. Then I glanced around to make sure everyone had gone. Sure enough, there were only the three of us in the room, so I told him how the detective had asked me about sleeping pills.

His eyebrows rose at that. "Somebody did away with the woman using sleeping pills and then stabbed her in the back? When she was already dead?"

"I'm not certain," I said. "Maybe they just gave her enough sleeping pills to make sure she was deeply asleep and then they stabbed her with the knitting needle."

He came forward and picked up my knitting. He took the needle that didn't currently have stitches on it, glanced at it and then at us. I knew what he was getting at. It didn't look very deadly.

He said, "If I did something like this, I'd be leaving a message."

"What do you mean?" Lucy asked.

He was still looking at the knitting needle as though he was considering how he would murder someone with it. "Well, I'd likely stab them to death first, and then I'd just pop the knitting needle in the hole. Otherwise, it's quite a bit of work." He tested the point of my knitting needle against his index finger. "And this one's not as sharp as I'd like."

I glanced at Lucy. "I didn't even really pay attention to what kind of knitting needle it was. Did you?"

She shook her head. "I saw a knitting needle sticking out of a woman's back. I didn't pay too much attention to what it was made of."

"Next time, perhaps you'll be more inquisitive," he said kindly, as though we were about to flunk detective school. I heartily hoped there would never be a next time. Still, I knew what he was saying. I wished I'd been more observant too. The shock had just blinded me.

He said, "I came to tell you that we're having a special meeting of the vampire knitting club tonight. I know you want this inconvenience to be cleared up as quickly as possible, Jennifer, and frankly, the fewer agents of the law are hanging about Shadowbrook Manor, the better. Let's give them their killer and they can be on their way."

I was heartily glad to know that the vampires were on board to help.

Lucy said, "We have a police officer staying with us. We can't just leave at ten o'clock at night."

He looked quite startled. "You have an agent of the law here?" He made to draw back into the shadows.

She shook her head. "He decided to go with the others to the pub. I don't think they were very happy to have him following them, but at least they were able to get out."

"And left you two undefended here?"

"We're not undefended," I reminded him. "There's Robin Trebilcock patrolling, Mr. and Mrs. Biddle living on the property, and Lucy and I do have some pretty good skills for protecting ourselves."

"Still, I don't like it. I can get one of my lads to come and stay for a few days, keep an eye on you if you'd like."

I could not think of anything worse. "Gryff, the police are going to wonder who the strange man is who just suddenly moved into the house. Thank you, but we'll be fine."

"Well, you've only to yell. You know one of us will be with you before your shriek is ended."

That made me think of something. "Did you hear a shriek last night? I wondered if she'd cried out when she died and no one had heard her."

"The lads and I were at sea, but Robin Trebilcock says he heard nothing and saw nothing untoward. And he's a sharp-eyed fellow, that one."

He glanced out the window as though making certain there was no one peering in at him and then said, "I'll be on my way. We meet at eleven upstairs in The Scallop Shell."

I spread my hands, feeling quite helpless. "I'd love to come, Gryff, but we can't get away without the police officer wondering where we're going."

He looked at me like I was being pathetic. "You won't be going out the front door. I shall come and collect you."

"Collect us from where?"

His eyes began to twinkle. "Did you really think a vampire would own Shadowbrook Manor and not have plenty of escape routes?"

I really hadn't thought about it, but of course it made sense. I just looked at him with my eyebrows raised, and with a grin, he headed over into an alcove. He lifted the rug, and I still couldn't see anything but polished floorboards. It wasn't until he bent down and lifted a section of the floorboard that I could see how cleverly the mechanism had been designed. The floor came up easily, and beneath it was a flight of stairs. I had seen enough of these in my short time with the vampires that I didn't even flinch. It did explain how I'd several times walked into the house to find Gryffyn standing in the living room staring out to sea. I'd assumed he had some supernatural way of coming and going, but now I understood.

I could see that there was lighting down there, but even so, I didn't think I'd be able to find my way to the shop. As though reading my mind, he said, "I'll come and collect you at eleven o'clock."

Lucy said, "I feel like one of us should stay here. Jennifer, you go."

I didn't like the idea of leaving her alone, but she reminded me of what I'd just said. We weren't helpless, Lucy and I. We had ways of protecting ourselves, and frankly one of us had better be on hand in case we had to protect our guests from a possible murderer.

Lucy gazed at both of us. "Here's what I don't understand. If the killer managed to stuff her full of sleeping pills, why shove the knitting needle in her back? It might have looked like a possible suicide, but adding that final wound makes it obvious she was killed."

I was staring at the spot that led down into the tunnel beneath us. "I'm worried that someone might see me. Just as they're coming home from the pub, they could glimpse me disappearing into the floor. I don't think that would look very good."

"Not to worry," Gryff said. "Most of the rooms have a way

out. Rafe hasn't survived for four hundred years without knowing where the back door is before he enters the front door of a dwelling."

"Do you know where the secret entrance would be in the apartment off the kitchen?" Was there one?

"Well, I'm sure I can find it." And so we took him through to the apartment where the former bed and breakfast managers had stayed. He didn't exactly nose around like a bloodhound, but he seemed to cast a pretty knowledgeable eye around the place, and then again, in another slightly recessed alcove where a small decorative table sat with a vase of silk flowers on it, he said, "Likely there."

It was the work of a minute for him to move the table out of the way, pull back the rug, and drop to his knees. Sure enough, there was another intricately inlaid wooden design, very similar to the one in the living room. He showed me how it worked and made me lift the cover myself to make sure I could get down there.

"It's brilliant," I cried. "What a work of engineering."

"Aye, Rafe would have hired the best craftsmen in the day. I'll pick you up then at eleven o'clock this evening."

I wished I had time for a nap. I was going to be tired tomorrow, but I really wanted the input of the vampires. I knew that, like Rafe in Oxford, Gryffyn had sources all over Cornwall. I said, "Any chance of finding out what the police know?"

He gave me a look as though I didn't even need to ask. He just nodded.

He said, "I'll meet you right down there at eleven."

"Thank you."

And then he said, "Mind you put the table back." And he

dropped down out of sight. Poof, like he'd never been there. Lucy made me show her the trick with the floorboard. We glanced at each other.

"You never know." She shrugged.

I absolutely agreed with her. We weren't vampires, but as Gryffyn had said, sometimes it was nice when you went into the front of a building to know where all your exits were.

We went back to the main lounge and continued knitting and chatting. We didn't talk about the murder anymore. I thought we'd both become a little overwhelmed by the topic, plus Lucy knew that I'd be immersed in the topic again once I got to The Scallop Shell.

She said, "You're sure no one will see lights on up there, are you?"

"Gryffyn says they've got extremely efficient blackout blinds. And I believe him."

The pub-goers arrived home in two batches, as they'd left. The older crowd arrived home about ten o'clock. I thought the outing had done them good. They all seemed a little less tense, and as they walked in, Maggie Cooper was laughing at something Nigel Hargreaves had said. It was good to hear laughter in the house again.

About half an hour later, Elliot and Issy returned. They weren't holding hands or anything, but I sensed that the evening had gone quite well for both of them, in spite of the circumstances.

The police officer was unobtrusive, returning just after Issy and Elliot, but we all knew he was out in the hallway. About ten minutes before eleven, I began yawning and said it had been a long day and I was going to head to bed. There was general agreement, and everyone then rose and began heading off to wherever they were sleeping. The police officer came in and explained that he'd be sitting upstairs in a chair if anyone needed him, and he would be relieved at midnight by the next shift. We thanked him, offered him a cup of tea, which he declined, and then Lucy and I headed into the apartment off the kitchen.

About one minute to eleven, I made sure the shutters were closed and the curtains drawn, and then, with a "Wish me luck," I moved the table away, pulled up the carpet, and opened the trapdoor. The tunnel below was lit, but still, it took some courage to step down onto rough-hewn wooden stairs, down below and into the ground. It was a weird feeling. It smelled dry enough but kind of airless and cool. At first it was too dark for me to make out anything but the stone walls and rough flooring.

"Gryffyn?" My voice came out high-pitched, more like a squeak.

"I'm here." His voice was so soothing in the dark. I felt better knowing he was nearby. And then like a shadow moving from against the wall, he came closer. "You're all right, lass," he said. Then he reached out and took my hand. It was cool and dry but comforting for all that. He led the way, and I followed. Maybe it was a little foolish, but I didn't let go of his hand.

I followed Gryff along the underground tunnel, trying very hard not to cling to his hand but very glad we were connected. There was no other word for it but creepy being down here. I felt as though I were in an underground labyrinth, which was probably true. Who knew how many of these interconnected tunnels, presumably some from the days of tin mining and some simply for the convenience of the vampires, existed down here? Well, if anyone knew, it was probably Gryff. I was reminded once again that there was the world above ground that I knew so well and then this entire shadow world that I was beginning to understand.

"Not much farther now," he said in a comforting tone, as though he could tell I was a little anxious. I was such a fool. Even if I wasn't clinging to his hand for dear life, he could probably tell that my heart rate was elevated. I suspected his vampire instincts were so keen that he knew how quickly my blood was pumping. I pushed that thought right out of my head. I knew that Gryff wouldn't hurt me, but being down in a dark tunnel in the dead of night with a vampire did not make me want to think about how fast my blood was pumping and that he could sense it. Definitely not going there.

At last I felt the footing underneath me change a bit, and it seemed as though the path traveled upwards slightly. And then he said, "Nearly there. You all right?"

"Yes." It wasn't entirely true, but I was putting on a brave face.

He said, "The stairs are just around that corner, and then you'll be coming up through the floor into your shop." A low chuckle shook him. "It will remind you of the day we first met."

I would never forget how terrified I was when I'd been in the shop facing down the cat that would turn out to be my familiar, but I didn't know that yet, when a piece of the flagstone floor lifted and up into what was supposed to be a disused shop came an eighteenth-century pirate. Incredible to think that the pirate was now someone I considered sort of a friend and that that bristling cat had become an important part of my life.

Sometimes when I considered the twists and turns my life had taken since I'd left Boston, they felt very much like these underground tunnels, twisting and turning in the darkness and I had no idea where I was going. I was trusting Lucy and fate the way I was trusting the vampire in front of me to get me where I was going.

True to his word, we turned the corner and I could see a rough-hewn set of stairs. He climbed ahead of me and then very gingerly eased the square of rock upward and peered out. He must have been satisfied, for he lifted the rest of the stone and pushed it to one side. I couldn't imagine the strength it must have taken to do that, but as I had already begun to note, vampires had a lot of powers, superhuman strength being just one of them.

There was quite literally a light at the end of this tunnel, and thankfully I climbed the stairs and took the hand he had outstretched to me. The last step was a bit of a hike, and then I found myself in my own knitting shop. It felt so familiar, I heaved a sigh of relief. I heard a meow and then Busby came scampering forward, nuzzling first Gryffyn and then me. I scooped her up in my arms and enjoyed the softness of her fur and the warmth of her body. She quickly began to purr and pushed her head up and bumped my chin.

Then Gryffyn said to her, "Don't look at me with such reproach, my darling. I've not had time to get your fish tonight. But it's coming, don't you worry."

She burrowed closer into me and purred more loudly. Gryff shook his head in comic despair. "She won't forgive me.

The one time I show up without a fish for her and she turns her back. Just like a woman."

I laughed at that. However old he might be, it seemed that men's attitudes to women never changed.

I quickly checked to make sure the blackout blinds were in place, which of course they were, and then the three of us —Busby, Gryffyn, and I—headed upstairs. I could already hear the low buzz of voices. And sure enough, when I got upstairs, I was surprised at how many vampires had packed into the relatively small space. More than I could recall ever seeing before.

A male vampire in a very intricate waistcoat looked somewhat out of place though familiar. Alfred said, "Jennifer, you remember Dr. Christopher Weaver? We asked him to come today, thought he might be of assistance."

"Yes, I remember you from Oxford," I said. "Thanks for coming."

"My pleasure. I like to be useful."

Gryff said, "Everyone wants to help solve this murder. The quicker we can get the authorities away from Shadowbrook Manor, the better for all of us."

Sylvia said, "And besides, Jennifer, we're very good at solving mysteries."

Beside her, Lucy's grandmother nodded. "That we are." And then she glanced around. "Won't Lucy be joining us?" She did look disappointed.

I explained that Lucy had stayed behind, as we had Shadowbrook Manor full of guests who might need something.

I didn't remind Lucy's grandmother that one of them might be a killer.

CHAPTER 16

"Good, now you're here, I think we're all assembled," Gwendolyn Poulsen said. She had gone full-on schoolmistress and was standing beside an easel with a large pad of paper on it. Very old-school, but she was clearly keen to run the meeting, and I had a feeling she'd be very good at it. Considering there were a lot of strong personalities in the room, I thought someone who had spent their career corralling students, some of whom had no doubt been very difficult, would be the perfect person to run this meeting.

Gryff hesitated for just a moment before saying, "Excellent, Gwendolyn, I see you've come prepared."

She dusted her hands as though they might have chalk on them, although of course there was no chalkboard, but she had provided herself with a series of multicolored felt pens. We settled ourselves in chairs that had been thoughtfully arranged so that we were in a double semicircle facing forward to where Gwendolyn stood. I suspected she had organized this herself and no doubt forced the other vampires to do the chair-moving. It was hard not to respect Gwendolyn Poulsen.

Dougan Hayes, the surfer, had taken a seat in the back semicircle as far from Gwendolyn as he could get and sat slumped, already looking bored. I suspected he'd fallen back into default mode, as Gwendolyn had no doubt reminded him of all the school days when he would have rather been out surfing than learning. It was interesting that Gwendolyn was the one who had turned Dougan into a vampire. I wondered if that made him more likely to do what she wanted.

Svanhilde had turned up and was sitting towards the outer end of the first circle, her friend Georgie beside her. She had said that she was the one who had turned Gryffyn, and he hadn't disagreed, and yet between those two, I didn't sense a closeness. It was almost slightly antagonistic. I wondered what that was about.

Then Gwendolyn said, "Now, if we are all present, I suggest we call this meeting to order." She turned and scanned the room. "Agnes, I wonder if you'd be kind enough to take the minutes?"

Agnes, who had been happily knitting, looked up and said, "Oh. Are we taking minutes?"

"I feel it's important if one is going to conduct a meeting of this nature that there should be some record, yes."

Agnes looked instinctively to Gryff, as did half the room. There was a little uncomfortable shuffling, and a voice said, "I don't want anything I say put down on any record." That was Robin Trebilcock, the gamekeeper. There was a murmuring of agreement.

Gryff spoke up then. "Gwendolyn, why don't we try this meeting without quite such formality. I believe that Jennifer here will take notes of anything important."

I nodded, appreciating that he had managed to appease the vampires who weren't comfortable with anything they said being written down, probably most especially their names, and Gwendolyn's desire to run a meeting in a proper fashion. Besides, I had fully intended to write notes of anything that seemed like it might be useful. I obviously wanted to share everything I learned with Lucy. Indeed, I had brought a notepad and pen for that purpose and picked it up and waved it around. That appeased Gwendolyn, who nodded sharply. But Robin Trebilcock looked very uncomfortable.

"What are you going to do with them notes?"

"Robin, I'm only going to share them with Lucy, who is Rafe Crosyer's wife, you know. I promise you they won't fall into the wrong hands."

He still looked uncertain. "Well, if I've anything to say, and I don't know that I do, mind, I don't want you using my name."

"Okay. Agreed. If I have to refer to you, may I use the initial R?"

He seemed to think about this. He narrowed his gaze at me as though I might have a trick up my sleeve and then finally nodded briefly. He mumbled to himself, "But I'll probably keep my trap shut."

I hoped the others were less concerned about me writing down things that happened in the meeting because I really needed their collective wisdom, experience, and any ideas they might have in this truly perplexing case. I wasn't a trained investigator; I wasn't even experienced like Lucy was. Still, I was determined to do whatever I could to help find justice for Anthea Fitzgerald. I sat in the farther back circle of chairs, mostly so that the vampires might forget that I was making notes, and Agnes moved her seat to sit beside me.

In a low voice, she said, "Don't worry, dear. Gwendolyn's very bossy, but she's efficient."

I leaned in and whispered, "I miss Lucy. She's so good at this."

Agnes tapped me with a knitting needle. "I miss Lucy, too. But you're an intelligent young woman. Just keep your mind open to new impressions."

That felt like something a witch would say to another witch, and of course Agnes had been a witch before she'd been turned. I knew immediately what she meant. It was too easy to follow in a straight line and miss the nuances. Like walking down a woodland path and staring at the ground and not hearing the birdsong or seeing the different foliage on the trees or smelling the lilac or hyacinth as you walked by. I suspected she was right and a murder investigation was very similar. There were the obvious facts of the case, but in a case as curious as this one, there had to be clues that were less than obvious that I might be able to pick up. Somehow those few words of hers gave me confidence, and I opened my notebook, clicked open my pen and waited.

Gwendolyn took the floor back. "Right. I suggest that Jennifer quickly recap for us what we know of this murder."

I'd been ready to take notes and maybe offer some suggestions, but I immediately felt put on the spot. I suspected they already knew more than I did anyway, but I did as she asked. I said, "It all started—"

Gwendolyn interrupted me. "Perhaps you could stand up, Jennifer. Then all the class can hear you."

I couldn't help but smile. No doubt all of us had noticed that she had used the word class. Still, perhaps it would be easier if everyone could see me, and I could make sure I was heard by all. Obligingly, I stood up. "I don't know much, but here's what I do know. Anthea Fitzgerald signed up to the knitting retreat. Lucy and I had met her in Oxford in a marketing class. She ran a small company and retail outlet in the Lake District with her own bath and beauty products, mostly skin creams, and claimed that they were all organic and natural and farmed close to where she lived and worked. However, it's possible that's not true." Then I explained about Margaret Twigg first suggesting that the ingredients Anthea claimed were in her products couldn't possibly have been grown near her and Nigel saying virtually the same thing.

Gryffyn spoke from beside me. "Do you have a sample of any of her products, Jennifer?"

"As a matter of fact, I do." I told him about the hand cream she'd given us in Oxford. I'd never used mine, but I knew I hadn't thrown it away. Then I told them that all of us retreat participants had been given a packet of her special herbal tea that she also sold, which was to help us relax and sleep better. I shrugged, "But that's back at Shadowbrook Manor."

"I'll come back with you and pick it up if you still have some about. And the hand cream."

"I do. I didn't want to drink any tea she made." I looked kind of apologetically around the room. "I'm sorry she's dead, but I didn't like her. Besides, if I need a calming tea to help me sleep, I can make my own."

There was a low chuckle from Agnes, and everyone else nodded.

I explained that Anthea had been killed the night before, and told them how I'd found her with a knitting needle sticking out of her back. Everyone stopped knitting and stared at me.

"A knitting needle in the back? How curious," Sylvia said.

"I know." I shuddered again at the memory. It was enough to put you off knitting.

"I once killed someone with a bodkin," Svanhilde reminisced fondly.

I wasn't even sure what a bodkin was, but in any case, Gryffyn said in a slightly reproving tone, "Perhaps we can focus on the killing of Anthea Fitzgerald."

Svanhilde looked slightly irritated. "As you wish, but this seems an awful lot of fuss for one dead day walker."

Well, this was going well. It was Gwendolyn this time who spoke up. "Nevertheless, Svanhilde, it gives us something to do, keeps our brains active. I for one am very intrigued to find out what happened to this Anthea Fitzgerald." And then she turned to the board and wrote at the very top in neat, precise handwriting, all capitals, "ANTHEA FITZGERALD," and then beside that she wrote, "Victim. Murdered by knitting needle stabbed in back."

I said, "The police were asking about sleeping pills, and two of the people who brought sleeping pills to the retreat found theirs were missing the morning of the murder. I don't know for sure, but it seems likely that someone stuffed a whole load of sleeping pills down Anthea Fitzgerald, so she was either dead or nearly dead when they drove the knitting needle into her back."

"But why would anyone do that?" Agnes wondered aloud.

"I'd say somebody's sending a message," Gryffyn said. "As Svanhilde pointed out, any of us could kill a mere mortal with a drawing pin most likely, but you day walkers don't have the strength or the skill."

He might be insulting my own kind, but I had to agree with him. "I wouldn't even know how to get a knitting needle between the ribs."

Svanhilde's eyes lit up. "Easier than you think, Guinevere. I can show you."

"No, thanks," I said quickly. Not a skill I really needed to know.

She looked a bit disappointed but went back to her work.

Dr. Christopher Weaver spoke up. "Gryffyn was able to obtain a copy of the autopsy report, and I can confirm an overdose of sleeping pills in her system. Her last meal was tofu and vegetables, and there were herbs in the stomach contents consistent with herbal tea."

"Was she already dead when the knitting needle went into her?" I wanted to know.

Christopher Weaver shrugged. "Difficult to know for certain. In any case, she had so much sedative in her, she'd not have felt it."

Gryff spoke up now. "The initial police report suggests there's no sign of forced entry. Either the killer had access to Shadowbrook Manor or, and I suspect we all believe this is more likely, one of the retreat participants killed Ms. Fitzgerald. Robin, you didn't notice any strangers around Shadowbrook Manor last night, did you?"

"No. It was all quiet when I did me rounds."

"What time was that?" I asked him.

"Midnight and again at three and five."

He was definitely thorough.

"When did Anthea Fitzgerald die?" Georgie asked.

Christopher Weaver didn't need to consult the autopsy report. "Between one a.m. and four a.m. is listed as approximate time of death."

Gwendolyn said, "Excellent work, Christopher and Gryff. Now, why don't we make a list of all the knitting retreat participants and see if we can start thinking of reasons why they might have wanted to take this person's life."

She'd made a few notes summarizing what I'd told her of Anthea and added notes about how she'd died.

She picked up a pen and turned to the page. "Jennifer, could you list the other participants and what you know of them?"

I wasn't sure what order to begin with. Did she want alphabetical order? The order in which they'd first registered? I decided that trying to arrange people alphabetically in my head was too complicated, so I told Gwendolyn that I would give her the names as I thought of them.

For some reason, I started with Lily Tang. "Lily is fifty," I told them. "She didn't put her age on the intake form."

"What woman would?" Sylvia asked.

"She's an accountant from Birmingham, and I can see no relationship between her and Anthea."

Gwendolyn made a few notes and said, "Next?"

Elliot. "Elliot Thomas. He's twenty-seven," I said. I explained that he was a recent fashion graduate, had learned knitting from his grandmother, and seemed to be very much enjoying Isabel's company.

"Can you think of any reason why Elliot Thomas might murder Anthea Fitzgerald?" Gwendolyn asked.

"No."

Then, because I had mentioned Isabel, I talked about her next. I said, "Isabel Sterling, twenty-eight." What to say about Isabel? I was surprised how very little I knew about her. Something about her had been bothering me from the beginning, so I just said it out loud. "Isabel, who goes by Issy, seems like she doesn't enjoy knitting. I really don't know why she signed up to a knitting and crochet retreat. She's a beginning knitter, and I don't think she has much desire to continue. Mostly she and Lucy just chat."

"Oh dear," said Agnes.

"No, it's fine. I think Lucy's enjoying the chats. She might be able to tell us more, but I think they talk about fashion, movies they've watched, and people they follow on Instagram more than sharing much about each other's lives. It's pretty clear Elliot has a crush on her."

"Do you think she returns the young man's interest?" This was Georgie, who hadn't spoken up much before but seemed very curious about what was going on. It was a good question.

"I'm not sure, but I think she likes him too." Then I told them I'd bumped into Issy downstairs around the time of the murder. "She said she was planning to make some tea in the kitchen, but they have kettles in their rooms. I suspected she might have been visiting Elliot." I explained that Elliot had moved downstairs because the snoring from his roommate Nigel was so terrible.

"Hmm," Gwendolyn said, tapping a capped pen on the paper in front of her. "We know she was awake when the woman was killed, then."

"But why would she want to kill Anthea?"

"That's the question we're trying to answer, Jennifer," she said to me, as though I were a remedial student who hadn't done my homework.

"Okay. I feel like she's hiding something," I said. I just put it out there. It was something I'd been thinking, and I didn't even know why except I had a strong feeling that Isabel Sterling had not come to the knitting retreat because she wanted to learn to knit.

"That's interesting," Sylvia said. Sylvia had been uncharacteristically quiet, possibly because she was working on a very intricate piece of lace. Now she glanced up. "It's very clear to me that someone on the knitting retreat murdered this woman, and I cannot imagine that there's been enough provocation in such a short time to invoke murder in their hearts. Therefore, the crime must have been premeditated. If this Isabel came to the knitting retreat not knowing how to knit and not wishing to learn, I think it would be prudent to look into her more carefully."

It made a lot of sense. I nodded. Gwendolyn made a note. "And of course we mustn't forget the young man was sleeping downstairs and presumably awake when the young lady came to visit him. Do we know why he's there? Does he have some ulterior motive?"

I said, "He seems like he's exactly who he says he is. But I guess if he wants to incorporate knitting into his fashion design, there's plenty of places in London he could have gone. He didn't have to journey to Cornwall for lessons."

Sylvia nodded sharply. "I agree with you, Jennifer. He would bear more looking into as well."

Gwendolyn spoke up now. "And what about this other man? The snoring one? What do we know about him?"

"Nigel Hargreaves is sixty-seven. He comes from the Lake District, as does Anthea." I felt like I knew more about Nigel than some of the others. He seemed quite forthcoming. I took a breath and really tried to take him in and gather my impressions together. I told them that Nigel Hargreaves learned to knit because his wife didn't drive and she was an avid knitter who loved to go to knitting retreats. Once he'd learned, the two of them used to go to knitting retreats together. "Now, tragically, she has dementia and lives in a care home." I thought about Nigel, pictured him walking in. "Oh, and Maggie Cooper and Rosalind Wallace, two of the other knitting participants, said they remembered his wife."

"Good, good," Gwendolyn said encouragingly. "And any entanglements with Anthea Fitzgerald that you know of?"

I shook my head. "They didn't seem to know each other. He did say that he thought she was a fake. That all her supposed care for the environment and ensuring that her ingredients were all organic and so on was probably untrue. He's a passionate gardener and lives in the same area as she does and is convinced she's lying about her ingredients being locally farmed." Then I heard the echo of my own words and corrected myself. "She *was* lying." I thought about it and said, "He seemed uncharacteristically vehement."

"Interesting. That would be worth checking out." The trouble was, so far it seemed worth checking everybody out.

Gwendolyn summarized what I had said about Nigel and then glanced over to me. She put a hand up to her face, and I got the feeling she'd have looked at me over her glasses, but of course now that she was a vampire, she didn't need glasses anymore. It must be an old habit from when she'd been a schoolteacher. I wondered if it felt good for her to be acting as though she were still a living schoolteacher. She seemed so enthusiastic that I suspected it was.

"You mentioned Maggie Cooper and Rosalind...Wallace, wasn't it? What can you tell us about them?"

CHAPTER 17

I nodded. It was interesting the way Maggie and Rosalind seemed to link naturally to the other. "Maggie Cooper is sixty-seven and was a professional librarian. She talks about a fancy private library that she worked in, in London. She was married to a barrister who died, and she's a brilliant knitter. She and Rosalind Wallace seem to bump into each other at a lot of knitting retreats, and it's pretty clear they have a strong rivalry. They're pleasant to each other on the surface, but they seem to enjoy baiting each other. Rosalind is seventy. She looks and acts exactly like a devoted grandmother. She's got six grandchildren and seems to spend all her time knitting for them. It's clear that she's deeply involved in their lives and seems to live for her family. She's been married for almost fifty years, she told us, and I don't think ever worked outside the home. Again, this is part of the rivalry between her and Maggie. Maggie never had children, which Rosalind often mentions, while Rosalind never had a career, which Maggie often mentions."

"That sounds petty and exhausting," Georgie said. "I was

a female professional athlete in a time when there weren't many of us, but it would have been tedious and in bad taste for me to look down on people who chose marriage and motherhood as their paths."

I nodded at her. "You're right. They also seem like they compete in the knitting projects. And they're both so good. But if Maggie shows off her original design, then Rosalind has to mention the intricacy of her work."

Agnes said, "If either Rosalind or Maggie was dead, it would be pretty clear who the culprit was, especially given the stabbing in the back with the knitting needle. But why would either of them kill Anthea Fitzgerald?"

She had me there.

Gwendolyn looked back at her list. "Who's left?"

"Sunita Rai," I said. "She's got an incredibly high-powered job in London and came very stressed out. She obviously wanted a peaceful week to simply knit. And Beatrice Huntington-Cole."

Sylvia glanced up at that. "Any relation to Rupert Huntington-Cole?"

I stared at her blankly, and she shook her head. "Never mind. Years before your time. One used to see him about town. Very dapper. Old money."

"I think Beatrice might have married his son or even grandson," I said, thinking that Beatrice's husband sounded like the man Sylvia had described.

"Beatrice Huntington-Cole. Beatrice didn't put her age, but I would put her somewhere in her sixties. She's glamorous and said she was knitting again to give her something to do since the death of her husband." I thought about Beatrice. "She's had bad luck with husbands. This was her fourth one who died."

Sylvia looked most interested by that. "Could she be a black widow? I played a woman like that on screen. It was a delightful part. She was really the most bloodthirsty villain and managed to put three husbands underground. She disposed of the fourth one by pushing him to his death at sea. But it was the fifth one when she was finally caught." She sighed rapturously. "My final scene before my character was hanged was particularly touching, if I do say so myself. A murderous woman, yes, but there was humanity in her too."

I had a feeling we were going to get an acting lesson if this went on much longer. I said, "Well, Beatrice did lose four husbands. Perhaps that is sort of excessive."

"Definitely worth checking out," Sylvia insisted.

"But why would that make her want to kill Anthea?"

"Perhaps Anthea knew what she'd done? Could she have threatened her in some way or tried to blackmail her?" This was Alfred's contribution.

"That's a very good point, Alfred," Gwendolyn said, making a note on the big sheet of paper.

There was silence as we all gazed at the large piece of paper with all these names and notes scribbled on it.

Anthea Fitzgerald's topped the list, larger than anyone else's name, but I didn't feel like we were any closer to figuring out what had happened to her.

Gryffyn spoke up then. "Did anything untoward occur in the time leading up to the murder? Anything mysterious or deadly? Was she warned in any way? Threatened? Was there an attempt on her life?"

I said, "There was one mysterious incident." And then I described how we'd gone to the Chinese restaurant and the fortune cookie had been opened by Beatrice. I was able to recite it from memory. "You will be killed in a very painful way. You know what you did."

"There, you see?" Sylvia cried. "Anthea must have sent that message to Beatrice Huntington-Cole. No doubt she knew that she'd murdered at least one of her husbands, and from what you've told us about the victim, she was willing to lie and manipulate for money. Blackmail doesn't seem like much of a stretch." Then she glanced at me, looking quite pleased with herself. "Dig deeper into the connection between Beatrice and Anthea, and I'm certain you'll find I'm right."

I wasn't quite as certain, but her theory was as good as any.

"Could Anthea have tampered with Beatrice's fortune cookie?" I liked that Christopher Weaver had the mind of a scientist. He wanted to make certain the logistics were possible.

I thought back to the evening of the dinner at The Lucky Pearl. "Yes. I think so. The fortune cookies were chosen by each of us from a basket, but we were passing food and pouring more tea, so I think everyone put theirs down on the table. It would be easy to reach over and replace one with another that had been tampered with."

"Hmm," Georgie said, looking up from the plaid sweater she was knitting. "That would require forethought and planning. The murderer would have had to know which restaurant you were going to, to have discovered there were fortune cookies, and to have somehow got hold of one."

"That's not difficult," Sylvia stated, very much in love with her own theory. "The killer could have stopped in for dinner before coming to the conference or simply gone in on some pretext or other. I'm sure the fortune cookies weren't under lock and key. Anthea could have stolen one or two and then made her threatening message."

Svanhilde nodded with enthusiasm. "And then this woman who murdered all her husbands discovered she did not wish to pay this blackmailer and killed her." She nodded. "This is a very sensible theory."

"Thank you, Svanhilde," Sylvia said, nodding her head graciously in the Viking's direction.

This was getting so convoluted, I wondered how anybody ever got convicted of murder. The police had my undying admiration.

Agnes held up her work. She was working on a knitted cushion cover. It was beautiful, like a field of wildflowers, each one so intricate and separate and yet part of the overall design. As she gazed at it, she said, "Patterns. We bring different threads and different colors together, and they all came from different places and have different histories, and then you stitch them together and there's a pattern." She turned to look at me. "I sense there's a pattern here. It may seem like these people came together in a random fashion, but I think if we look deeper, we will find the pattern, and that will lead us to the killer."

If I was going to continue with her metaphor, all I could see was a tangle, and I felt like if I pulled on any one of the threads, I'd just turn the whole thing into a knot. And yet how did you undo a knot? You teased the different threads apart. I nodded.

I stood up and went to the board. To Gwendolyn, I said, "May I?" and at her nod of permission, I took a colored pen. I drew a line from Beatrice to Anthea. "Possible black widow? Did Anthea know something?" I turned to Christopher Weaver. "Would you be able to discover what Beatrice Huntington-Cole's husband died of?"

"Certainly. If he died at home, there would be an autopsy and a report. I'll have it to you in the morning."

"Thank you. And if it's possible to find out about her other husbands?" I tapped the pen on the page. "The police must have looked into it if she had four husbands die on her."

He nodded. "If I can't access all the records, Rafe will know who can."

"Excellent." But I didn't want this to be our only line of inquiry.

I came back to Anthea again. "If she lied about her products, which we all think she did, why would someone kill her for that? Is that a possibility?" To Gryffyn, I said, "When you get that cream analyzed, can you please find out if there's anything that could potentially be toxic in some way? I mean, I feel like if someone else had been lying about their natural products and using suspect ingredients, it might have given Anthea a reason to kill. But if she was doing it, who would kill her over that? Still, I think we should look into it."

Gryff nodded. "You'll have the results in the morning."

That was the great thing about vampires: They worked cheerfully all night. No doubt there was some lab somewhere that would be very busy for the next few hours.

Other threads. I thought about what Agnes had said. What were they? How did they connect back? I looked down at each of the names. One jumped out at me. As Agnes had said, when I allowed my senses to open fully and my instincts to operate in a more intuitive way, something else began to emerge. I came down to Nigel Hargreaves, and as Gwendolyn had done, I tapped the capped pen against his name.

"He was quite annoyed about the way he was convinced she had lied about the ingredients in her creams. It seemed more personal."

"But obviously he was not harmed," Sylvia said. I thought she was feeling miffed that I hadn't ended the investigation when she came up with the Anthea/Beatrice scenario.

"Yes, he was." I tapped harder. "The person he loves most in the world is his wife. Could she have somehow become incapacitated by the ingredients in those creams? Could they have caused her dementia or sped it up?" Even as I said it, I thought that was a pretty far-fetched theory. But there was something there. I was sure of it.

Gryff spoke up again. "If you can give me the woman's name and the facility where she's living, I'll learn everything I can."

I appreciated that very much. He didn't make me feel stupid for flinging out a far-fetched theory. He seemed to think that it was worth at least investigating, even if we discounted it later.

There was silence, and I felt that the vampires were probably eager to get on with their night's activities. This was the time of night when they did their visiting and entertainments. I knew that the surfer would want to get out surfing, and the seafarers would want to get out seafaring. Agnes and Sylvia had loads of friends in Cornwall and would no doubt get Alfred to drive them in the Bentley on a round of visiting. I would lose them soon. What else did I want to know? What else could they work on while I was hopefully sleeping?

And then Georgie spoke up. "What about these two

young ones? I think there's something going on there." We all turned to look at her. She leaned forward and said, "You said they showed up together, and Elliot claimed that he had picked up Isabel from the bus stop because she was holding a knitting bag, and so he assumed she was coming to the knitting retreat. That seems rather convenient to me. They pretend they don't know each other, but they arrive together. Then you found her downstairs where he was sleeping in the middle of the night. I think there's more going on with those two than meets the eye."

I was willing to go along with her. "But what?"

She shrugged. "I don't know. Maybe they're in it together. Maybe they both hated Anthea Fitzgerald for some reason. And it does seem that this could be a crime committed by two people."

That was true. We seemed to have plenty of suspects but no plausible motives. I asked Georgie if she had any way of finding out more about Elliot Thomas and Isabel Sterling.

Alfred, who had been so quiet during the meeting I'd suspected he was daydreaming, spoke up suddenly. "I may be able to help there. Also, do we know the first name of Nigel Hargreaves's wife?"

I took a second to think back to earlier conversations and was pretty sure Nigel had said his wife was named Joan. Alfred nodded and made a note. "Does she have the same surname? Is she Joan Hargreaves?"

I didn't know for sure, but I thought since they'd been married for so long that it was a reasonable guess.

Alfred said, "You'll remember young Hester, Jennifer, from Oxford. She's become such a proficient at computer research that there's very little she can't find out for you.

Can you send me everything you know about this Nigel Hargreaves? And anything you can recall he's mentioned about his wife. I'll send it straight over to Hester, and I think you'll be surprised how quickly you'll find out anything there is to know about Mrs. Hargreaves. She'll also be able to find out a great deal regarding Isabel Sterling and Elliot Thomas. If it wouldn't be stepping on your toes, Georgie?"

"Please, step away," she said. "I didn't have a clue how I was going to find out anything about those two. Your Hester sounds wonderful."

I was thrilled by this idea. I hadn't yet worked out what the Cornwall vampires were capable of, and certainly I knew that Hester was brilliant at computer research. I suspected she was also a proficient hacker.

I said, "Do you think she can get into Joan Hargreaves's medical records?" Okay, I was clearly perfectly aware that that kind of information wasn't just lying around on the Internet.

Alfred looked down his long nose at me as though I'd said something particularly stupid. "Oh yes," he said.

I told him I would send him all the information I had from Nigel Hargreaves's initial application form for the knitting retreat, which of course included his home address. I'd also ask Lucy in case she remembered anything about his wife that I didn't. Like, for instance, where her care home was situated.

Then I said, "While Hester's looking, can you see if she can find any connection between Nigel Hargreaves and Anthea Fitzgerald? They both lived in the Lake District, but it would be interesting to see whether we can find a link to them buying product from Anthea that might have made Joan's dementia worse."

Svanhilde had been knitting at incredible speed. Now she stopped and glanced up. "Is this not what you British would call a wild goose chase? Some cream some woman made might have made another go funny in the head? This is how you solve crime?"

I knew I was on thin ice, but I didn't think it was fair of her to make me feel so stupid about a line of inquiry. Before I could even try to defend myself, Gryff spoke up.

"Svanhilde, you of all people know that this isn't chasing wild geese so much as when you're out fishing and you would cast your net wide; your aim might be to catch herring, but in your net you will gather all sorts of irrelevant fish that you would throw back. That's what we're doing here. Not all of these little fishing expeditions will bring in anything useful, but you might be surprised what turns up. Perhaps you were after herring but caught a particularly delicious eel."

She made a noncommittal grunt and went back to her knitting.

I'd been watching Svanhilde work a single needle with incredible speed, but I still hadn't been able to work out what it was she was working on. Finally, I asked her.

"Svanhilde, what is it that you're making?"

She turned to stare at me. "I am Nalbinding, making proper woolen slippers. They are very warm. Good even when at sea."

I looked at her, already back at work. "Do you sail your Viking ship now?" I knew that Gryff and his crew went out at night. I wondered if Svanhilde did the same.

She shook her head. "Those days are long behind me. But it is pleasant to have proper footwear about me."

She seemed so satisfied with herself, and I thought so long as she kept making her fancy slippers, she'd stay out of trouble. And out of my business.

We finished the meeting with pretty much everybody having been assigned a task. Gryffyn and Hester, via Alfred, had the most timely and the most important ones to do.

The vampires all slipped away, either out the door or through the downstairs trapdoor. Busby slipped out the door when Alfred, Agnes, and Sylvia left together.

Gryffyn held back until the last of them had gone, and as tired as I was, I didn't mind waiting. I wanted to make sure my shop was cleared of vampires before my assistant came in to open for business the next morning.

When they'd gone, he said, "Thank you for that, Jennifer."

I felt surprised. Shouldn't I have been thanking him? "For what?"

"The sleuthing. It's engaged us all, given us something useful to do. And, I'll be frank with you, you'll be accepted by the group much more quickly if you can capture their interest."

CHAPTER 18

*A*fter everyone had left and I'd made sure there was no sign the vampires had even been there, Gryff lifted the flagstone trapdoor thing and indicated that I should go first. I'd have preferred he go first, but then of course he'd have had to climb back up to put the flagstone back in place, so I stopped being such a baby and made my careful way down the staircase into the tunnel.

He didn't leave me down there alone for very long. I heard the scrape as the stone settled back into place, and then he was beside me. Once more, he held my hand. I didn't need it so much this time, but I didn't pull away either. Was this a friendship we were developing?

Gryffyn was growing on me. I could see that beneath the devil-may-care attitude of a dispossessed younger son who turned to piracy was a strong moral code. It might be different from mine, but I was fairly certain that in his way, Gryffyn cared about justice. And even if it was just a hobby to help solve crime, I could see that he was fully engaged.

When we got back to Shadowbrook Manor and Gryffyn

had made sure there was no one but Lucy there, we both climbed up into the apartment where she and I were staying. I'd wanted to be quiet in case she was sleeping, but she wasn't. She was fully dressed, and Busby had obviously beaten us home. The two of them were sitting, Busby curled up on Lucy's lap, while Lucy worked on something on the computer. She looked both delighted and relieved to see us.

"How did it go? Please tell me you figured out who killed Anthea Fitzgerald."

I shook my head. "I'll share with you what we came up with." I had taken the pages off the easel and had them with me so that I could share them with Lucy. She'd been solving crimes longer than I had, so I hoped she might offer some good insights. Maybe she'd look at the pages with all the names and notes and she'd see the pattern that none of us had been able to.

As I unfolded the papers and spread them out on the floor, I said, "You take a look at these and see what you think." Then to Gryff, I said, "Give me a second and I'll find that cream."

"What cream?" Lucy wanted to know. I told her that we were going to have the hand cream that Anthea Fitzgerald had given us at the digital marketing class in Oxford analyzed to see if there was something horrible in it that might have given Nigel Hargreaves's wife dementia.

Her eyes widened slightly and, although she was much more polite about it than Svanhilde had been, I could see that she was pretty skeptical that this would be the answer to Anthea's murder. However, what she did say was, "I've got my tube in my handbag."

That saved me digging through the box of rarely used

cosmetics and hair products that I kept underneath the sink in my room, which was currently occupied by Beatrice Huntington-Cole.

She said, "I've used it once or twice, but I really don't like it." She pulled it out and handed it over to Gryffyn. "It makes my hands itch."

He uncapped the cream, closed his eyes and waved the tube back and forth under his nose. Vampires do have extremely good senses of smell. He wrinkled his nose and said, "Underneath a pungent, almost offensive profusion of lavender, I smell formaldehyde and other chemicals I cannot recognize. It will be interesting indeed to find out what the chemical composition is of this."

"So you don't think it's all natural and organic?"

He gave a short laugh. "I'd bet a sack full of doubloons it isn't."

Since he tended to carry a sack of gold doubloons around with him and it amounted to a small fortune, I took his answer seriously.

I also gave him the tea that I had never bothered to brew, and with a brief nod, he disappeared back down into the tunnels.

I told Lucy to keep thinking and to scribble any notes she thought would be useful right onto the pages that I'd just brought up from the meeting. While she did that, I pulled up Nigel Hargreaves's form that he'd filled out and prepared to email it to Alfred. But before I did so, I asked Lucy if she could remember anything about Nigel Hargreaves's wife, in particular where her home was located or if they shared the same last name.

Lucy closed her eyes. Then she opened them. "I think he

said the home was in Windermere, not far from where he lived in Ambleside."

"And Anthea lived in Keswick. Is that far from Ambleside?"

Lucy scrunched up her nose. "Nothing's very far away in the Lake District. It's not like the States."

Right. I still tended to forget that I was on a relatively small island.

Then she reminded me that the wife had been in finance and lost most of their money. I wasn't sure if it was useful, but I added it all to the email, and then I sent it off to Alfred.

I told her that Alfred's idea was to get Hester on the case, and Lucy nodded with enthusiasm. "Hester has her issues, but she's brilliant."

Now the two of us sat and gazed at the notes from the meeting. "I wish you'd been at the meeting," I told her. "Especially when I came up with things that were slightly outrageous. I think I would have felt less foolish if you were there too."

"Definitely. I would have encouraged you. It's amazing how sometimes the strangest idea leads to something you wouldn't have thought of otherwise. I don't think we've ever actually said that there are no stupid or crazy ideas, but it's how I see things."

That made me feel much better.

It was almost two in the morning by this time, and fatigue was pulling at us. Busby had disappeared into my bedroom, where no doubt I would find her sound asleep on my bed.

I could tell that Lucy was perturbed about something, so before bidding her good night, I asked, "What is it, sister?"

Her frown deepened. "I don't even like to say this, but I

feel like there's danger in this house. I can't explain it, but I'm worried."

I didn't even attempt to talk her out of her feelings and tell her she was overreacting. I sat down again. "I thought it was just the residual darkness from Anthea's violent death under this roof."

"So you feel it too?" she said, not eagerly, exactly, but in a resigned way, as though she had hoped I would tell her she was being silly.

"I do."

We looked at each other with concern. She said, "The chances are pretty high someone in this house took Anthea's life. Do you think that's what we're feeling?"

I shook my head slowly. "You used the word danger. I can't stand to even say it, but is it possible we have a serial killer under our roof?"

She shook her head like crazy so her blond curls bounced. "Don't even say that. And besides, I don't think so. There's a deep unhappiness and a longing as well as dark anger. That's what I'm feeling."

Considering that Lucy hadn't even known she was a witch while I'd been practicing for years and years, sometimes she impressed me with how very good she was. I'd been so busy focusing on who had killed Anthea Fitzgerald and why that I'd pretty much blocked out a lot of the shock and fear and buzziness of the other people in the knitting retreat who were still staying here. But if I closed my eyes and opened my senses, I could feel it too.

"We've got that police officer staying in the house," I said. "Surely no one would attempt another murder while he's here."

Lucy shrugged helplessly. "I hope not."

"Well, there's nothing else we can do tonight but get some rest. Blessed be," I said to her. She returned the greeting and then disappeared into her own room.

I got into bed and was happy to have Busby curled up beside me. Lucy was right. There was a feeling in the house that made me very worried. Was it possible that the killer would strike again? But if that was so, then all those motives that we'd come up with were useless. It would mean that there was some hitherto unknown connection between Anthea Fitzgerald and someone else in the knitting group that put them in danger as well. Or was that even true? I wished I knew more about everybody staying under this roof. Maybe there was a way to get them all talking and hope against hope that the killer would unmask themselves.

So long as we were stuck here anyway and using our time to knit, maybe I could start steering the conversation in more useful directions. With luck, someone would get comfortable enough to accidentally say the thing that would make it clear they had evil intentions, certainly to Lucy and me, who had sharper instincts than most. It was all I could hope. And while I tried to think of innocuous-sounding comments that would provoke a killer to unmask themselves, I fell asleep.

IT WAS a tired and ragged-looking bunch who gathered around the breakfast table the next morning. I was relieved to see that everyone was accounted for. I didn't think I could have borne another trip upstairs to find a dead knitter. The police officer who had spent the night was relieved by a new officer, who also refused a cup of coffee and chose to sit in the lounge while we were still at breakfast around the big table in the dining room. Even though we had the breakfast room, for some reason we had begun eating around the big table and it had just continued.

Agatha showed up for breakfast. I so appreciated that she kept turning up. She didn't have to, because she hadn't been on the premises at the time of the murder, so the police couldn't possibly force her to come here, but I felt there was a kind of solidarity with me as a fellow Tregrebi shopkeeper, and perhaps there was a curiosity to see how this thing would play out.

Even Mrs. Biddle seemed to have softened now that Agatha had not deserted us in our time of need. She even quite pleasantly said, "I hope you slept well, Agatha."

"I did, thank you, Ellen. Very well indeed."

It was such a breakthrough from the frosty way they'd communicated before that I felt at least one good thing had come out of this disaster.

I was trying to think of a subtle way to find out more about Nigel Hargreaves's wife when Maggie Cooper asked Nigel Hargreaves to pass her the marmalade. As she scooped some of Mrs. Biddle's homemade marmalade onto her plate and then began to spread it onto her toast, she said, "Have you heard anything about your wife while you've been here? Is all well with her?"

Nigel looked quite pleased at the question. "I have, thank you. I phone the nursing station every day. They say she's doing fine. I suppose that's all I can ask. She doesn't seem to know that I'm not coming every day."

He looked quite sad and stopped speaking. Maggie said,

"I thought, with your permission, I might go and visit her one day."

He looked quite surprised at that. "Really, Maggie? That's most kind of you."

"Well, we've knit together on many an occasion. I thought perhaps if I sat with her and knit for a while, it might be soothing."

"That's most kind of you," he repeated.

"Whereabouts is her home located again?"

"It's the Caring Hands Centre in Windermere," he said. "But tell me before you go so I can prepare her for your visit."

"Of course." She spread marmalade on a second piece of toast. But she'd yet to begin eating the first. As the golden marmalade slid onto the toast, she said, "She's always struck me as a very interesting woman. She was so modest. I remember you said she worked in finance. What exactly did she do?"

"Joan worked in international finance until she retired. She handled all our investments and was extremely good at it." He sighed. "Until she became incapacitated. If only I'd known what she was doing, but I thought she was simply becoming forgetful."

This was absolutely amazing. These were the kinds of details that I had hoped to winkle out. Maggie seemed to be doing my job for me and in a much smoother way, because she'd actually known Joan Hargreaves, so her questions were natural.

And then I began to wonder, were they natural? As Maggie Cooper had been very quick to tell all of us, she was a high-level librarian. Weren't librarians also researchers? Was she taking a hand in the sleuthing? Or was there something more sinister at work here? Maggie Cooper wasn't really a suspect on our list, because we couldn't find a reason why she would have killed Anthea Fitzgerald. Her sudden interest in Mrs. Hargreaves could spring from a genuine desire to visit the woman and hopefully bring some pleasure into her day even if she did quickly forget it, or it could be something more sinister. Whatever the case, I tried to memorize everything she said so that I could pass it on to Alfred to pass it on to Hester.

We were doing our best to act as normal as possible when Lily Tang suddenly said, "Would anyone be willing to change rooms with me? I cannot stand my room being beside that of poor Anthea Fitzgerald. I think about her being murdered within feet of me, and I can hardly bear it. I shall go mad if I don't get some sleep."

There was a deathly silence. I felt like nobody wanted to change places with her. I glanced over at Lucy, and I thought one of us was going to have to offer our beds when Nigel Hargreaves spoke up.

"I'd be happy to swap rooms with you, if it's all right with you, Mrs. Biddle?"

The housekeeper nodded stiffly. "I'm changing all the beds today anyway. It makes no mind to me."

Lily looked extremely relieved. Then Nigel Hargreaves turned to Elliot. "That's assuming you don't mind, old chap? I know you haven't been sharing my room anyway because of my dreadful snoring."

Elliot said it was fine with him. I had a feeling he'd come to quite like staying down on this level.

Nigel Hargreaves gave a firm nod. "That's settled, then."

Lily looked at him. "But won't you be bothered?"

"No more bothered than I am being a few doors down. No. I don't believe in ghosts, if that's what you mean."

"I can't explain it. It's just this awful feeling I get."

I could have explained to her what was going on. If I so much as walked by that room, I felt the darkness of death. It was dissipating, but it was still heavy in the room.

It crossed my mind that the one person who would be least bothered by sleeping in the room next to the one where the murder victim had gasped her last would be the one who had taken her life. Then I realized that was just unkind. Nigel Hargreaves was obviously trying to do a nice thing. I should leave it at that.

When breakfast was over, we all retreated to our rooms to brush our teeth and get ready for the day and retrieve our knitting. When I walked in, I wasn't particularly surprised to see Gryffyn sitting at the table with a delighted-looking Busby just licking her whiskers.

"Did you give her a fish?"

"Of course I did. You know I always feed her fish."

He was delicately wiping his fingers on a linen napkin. What could I say? He'd been giving Busby fish long before I'd met either of them, and she seemed to be thriving on it. I tried to round out her diet by giving her other cat food that would contain all the other nutrients she needed. It seemed like a reasonable compromise.

"Do you have any news for me?" I asked.

"Naturally. That's why I'm here." Then he sent me a devilish look. "That and to visit my darling, of course." Since he sent a glance to Busby, I had to laugh. However, he took an official-looking report from his pocket and passed it over to me. "That is the chemical analysis of the hand cream."

I could see lines and lines of ingredients, and some of them were highlighted in yellow with handwritten notes beside them.

"I don't even know what most of this means. But it doesn't look very good."

"There's a full precis at the end, but I'll sum it up for you. That hand cream was not manufactured in this country. It was made in a factory where there are none of the regulations that exist in the UK, the EU, or any nation that cares about the health of its people. There are ingredients that have been banned in this country for decades, many because they're cancer-causing."

I was absolutely shocked. "And that's the product that Anthea was handing around saying was organic and grown close to home?" I'd suspected she was stretching the truth, but this was appalling. Beyond anything I could have imagined. "Is it possible that some of these ingredients would have caused dementia?"

"You'd need an expert for that, but I think it's entirely possible. But are you absolutely certain that Mrs. Hargreaves purchased cosmetics from Anthea Fitzgerald?"

I shook my head. "No. But it's a theory."

He nodded. "I'll leave you to read the report, but what you'll see is it would take quite a bit of the product rubbed into the skin over a fair amount of time for a possible dementia to occur."

I tapped the paper angrily against the table. "Why would she do that? Why would she lie?"

"I can tell you that unscrupulous people often lie if it's to their own advantage. Bringing in creams from factories like these costs a fraction of what it would cost to make her own.

And she was a small enough operator that she was able to get away with it."

"I didn't like her very much, but I am truly shocked that she had stooped so low. A woman who would go around wearing hemp clothing and refusing to eat an egg was poisoning her customers? What kind of unscrupulous and unsafe work practices were going on in that factory?"

"She was a hypocrite indeed. But is that what motivated someone to kill her?"

I tapped the paper against the table again. "Isn't that the question? I need a list of all of Anthea's customers for the last five years," I said. "It makes sense that living in the Lake District, Joan Hargreaves might have visited Anthea's shop and bought some cream. Perhaps she kept using all her chemical-laden creams thinking she was helping a local business and promoting her own health when she was doing anything but."

CHAPTER 19

*W*hen I came back, everyone was sitting in a circle in the main living area, including Issy and Lucy, who'd given up any pretense that they were doing a beginner's lesson. Elliot sat beside Isabel, and there was a closeness between them that was kind of sweet. Then I looked around the group again. Everyone was there except for Maggie Cooper.

"Where's Maggie?" I asked.

Rosalind said, "She asked to be excused for an hour or so. She said she had some emails to send."

I nodded. It was normally Sunita who needed to take a break from knitting in order to answer business email, but I could understand that Maggie, like the rest of us, had people she had to keep in contact with. I wondered if she'd been confiding in someone about the murder.

I gazed at each of the knitting participants in turn. One of them was a murderer—I was certain of this—but which one? Grandmotherly Rosalind Wallace, of whom I could think of nothing more negative to say except she boasted constantly about her grandchildren? She lived for her family. How could the woman who was even now choosing between crayon-colored duckies and puppies for the buttons on the latest sweater she had knit for her grandson be a murderer?

Next to her was Sunita Rai, her brow furrowed in concentration as she worked on her scallop shell sweater in crochet. She worked so hard in London that she'd come here to relax, but she couldn't have chosen a less relaxing way to spend a week. She was another one that I couldn't find a motive for. Was I wrong? Had I not looked hard enough?

Lily Tang had come from Birmingham in order to knit. I suspected she also used knitting as stress relief. Could she have known Anthea Fitzgerald and come to hate her enough to kill?

I was still struggling over these suspicions when Mrs. Biddle came towards me and, leaning in, said in a confidential tone that she'd like to speak to me in the kitchen.

Naturally, I immediately panicked and wondered what I'd done to incur the housekeeper's displeasure. I rose as nonchalantly as I could, running through a mental list of possible things I'd done to displease Mrs. Biddle as I followed her into the kitchen.

Then she turned. "There's a gentleman to see you, miss. In your own apartment he is."

"Ah, thank you, Mrs. Biddle." I went into the apartment, and there was Alfred standing in the middle of the living area. I did not think he'd be here if he didn't have some news for me and greeted him, waiting impatiently to hear what he had to say.

Alfred glanced about to make sure no one else was listening. "Hester's been very busy."

I knew he had news. There was a sort of suppressed excitement about him. I felt my heartbeat quicken. "And?"

"I'm sorry to say that Nigel Hargreaves's wife, Joan, has suffered indeed at the hands of Anthea Fitzgerald."

I appreciated that he was enjoying stretching out the drama and making me wait, but come on. I leaned forward and grasped his forearm. "Was she one of Anthea's customers? Was she buying one of the more toxic creams?"

He shook his head slowly. "She was investing money in the woman's business."

My eyes widened at that. "What?"

He nodded slowly. Full of import. "To the tune of two hundred thousand pounds."

I felt fury stir in my chest on behalf of a vulnerable woman who'd been taken advantage of by a genuinely unscrupulous person. "I know her husband said that she had made some bad investments. I had no idea. Two hundred thousand pounds. That's a lot of money. I don't suppose she got any of it back?"

He shook his head. "There was no proper paperwork. When Mr. Hargreaves tried to get it back, Anthea Fitzgerald claimed it was a gift. With no paperwork, he couldn't find a lawyer to take the case. They suggested it was a criminal case, but I doubt the police would have had the resources to follow up."

"But the woman who invested money was diagnosed with dementia."

Again he looked sad. "I suspect that she didn't make it known. She was targeted and preyed on by an unscrupulous person, that much is clear. But how to prove it? Joan Hargreaves had a history of investing in companies she believed in. She could simply have made a mistake."

I felt my fingers curl in fury at how Joan Hargreaves had been preyed upon by Anthea. If no one would fight to get the money back, I could sympathize with Nigel's fury and desire to get back at Anthea in whatever way he could, though I hoped in his place that I'd have stopped short of murder.

Alfred then handed me a sheaf of papers printed from a computer. "This is everything Hester could find on your knitters and crocheters. A lot of it is standard stuff from their online profiles and so on. The only one she can't find is Isabel Sterling."

That startled me. "Really?"

Alfred nodded. "I was surprised too. It seems to be it's the young people who have profiles all over social media, where they post everything from their beauty routines to their deepest secrets." I had to smile. How long did Alfred spend online? "Even Rosalind Wallace has a big online presence, posting photos of her grandchildren and her knitting. Why would such a young person not have a single profile?"

"Perhaps she values her privacy," I suggested.

"Or she doesn't exist."

I felt like no sooner did one path to the answer of Anthea's murder seem lit up than another opened. Who was Isabel Sterling? And why might she have wanted Anthea Fitzgerald dead?

Alfred continued, "Gryffyn Penrose said you wanted a list of all Anthea Fitzgerald's customers from the past five years?"

"Yes."

He handed me another printed list. I couldn't believe how quickly Hester had worked her magic.

I didn't know why I'd asked for customers going back that far. Perhaps because, in our marketing course, we'd been asked to plan ahead in five-year chunks of time.

That made me think about my own life. Where would I be in five years?

A shiver crawled up my spine. I had a bad feeling that somewhere in that time I'd have to confront Vincent Blackwood. The sorcerer had found me psychically. It would only be a matter of time before he found me physically, if he hadn't already.

He'd frightened me away from my home once. I was determined he wouldn't do so again.

Alfred pulled me back to the present moment. "You've got something in mind."

I couldn't exactly explain the vague sense I had, so I simply nodded. "As you know from our last meeting, sometimes I get these wacky ideas, but you never know when you've hit on the right one."

He smiled slightly. "I can see why you and Lucy have been friends for so long. You have a very similar approach to life and detection work."

I was secretly delighted that first, he thought Lucy and I were alike, and second, that he called this crazy thing we did late at night genuine detection work. I felt like Sherlock Holmes, Miss Marple, and Nancy Drew rolled all into one. I just hoped I'd have any kind of the success those three enjoyed.

I scanned the list of customers, not even sure what I was looking for, when a familiar name jumped out at me.

My eyes widened as I stood there, trying to figure out what it could mean.

CHAPTER 20

a s I crossed the hall back to where everyone was about to break off knitting to pause for tea, I noticed Maggie Cooper talking quietly to the police officer who was keeping an eye on us all.

When she came into the dining room and sat at the table, Rosalind said, "You were an awfully long time. Had lots of email to send, did you?"

Maggie looked embarrassed that her friend had mentioned how long she'd been gone. She blushed slightly and then shook her head. "I found I had more to answer than I had imagined." And she smiled slightly. "I do still help other younger librarians, you know, when they are stuck on research."

"You're a research librarian?" Nigel said, looking interested.

She glanced at him and glanced away quickly, almost to her plate. She responded, "All good librarians are researchers."

He nodded. "I suppose that's true. I remember once trying

to find out the history of the street where I lived. I didn't even know where to start. I'd heard rumors that William Wordsworth had once stayed in the house where I was living but had no way of confirming it. It was the local librarian who worked it out for me."

Elliot looked at him. "And did he?"

Nigel put down his knife and fork and raised his eyebrows. "I beg your pardon?"

Elliot said, "And did he? Did William Wordsworth stay in your house?"

Nigel shook his head. "Sadly, no. I believe Coleridge drank at the local pub, but that's not quite the same thing, is it?"

We all agreed that it wasn't. There was a lull in the conversation.

I was going to suggest we plan a show and tell for the afternoon when the doorbell rang. The police officer on duty answered it, and in walked the two detectives, DI Barnsley and Sergeant Frances Draycott.

I felt rather than saw that there was police backup in the foyer.

Oh, dear. The level of nervous tension around the lunch table rose faster than a child's temperature during flu season.

"Don't get up," DI Barnsley said as Nigel began to rise. He took a seat at the head of the table so we could all see him, and his detective stood to the side, her notebook out.

"Have you come to make an arrest?" Lily asked, then blushed hotly as though mortified at voicing the question on all our minds.

"We'll have to see, Ms. Tang." Then he settled back in his chair and sighed. "This has been a peculiar case from the beginning. Why would someone stab a woman in the back with a knitting needle when she'd have died of an overdose of narcotics anyway?"

He gazed blandly at us, and Elliot answered. "Because it was personal."

"Exactly," DI Barnsley said. I felt that he was enjoying himself and no doubt making the murderer squirm. Was he hoping to provoke a confession?

If so, none was forthcoming.

"But who would kill someone at a knitting retreat?" He was met with silence. It wasn't like we hadn't all asked ourselves these questions.

"And more to the point, why?" DI Barnsley seemed like he was a fisherman who liked to tire his prey before reeling it in. He glanced around at everyone at the table, and I think for a moment we all searched our consciences in case we might have done it. Then he said, "Murder investigations usually begin with the victim. Who was this person? What can we gather about them?" He waved a hand around the table. "Anthea Fitzgerald, from what I can gather in talking to all of you, acted like she was almost too good to be true."

It was interesting how many times I'd had that thought myself.

He continued, "She was a vegan, allegedly only used the purest of ingredients in her products, and sounded very much like a woman of strong principle and virtues."

Sunita was nodding.

The detective continued, "Sadly, that was not the case. We've discovered that Ms. Fitzgerald was in financial trouble and that there wasn't much she wouldn't stoop to if it allowed her to keep her shop going, whether through determination or pure ego or some combination of both. The more we've investigated Ms. Fitzgerald, the more a second image arose of an unscrupulous manipulator who hid behind the virtuous persona."

I felt queasy at those words. Not because they weren't true but because they were. I'd known I didn't want her here. Why hadn't I made up some excuse as to why she couldn't come to the retreat?

Then he turned to Nigel Hargreaves, who'd been listening with interest. "Mr. Hargreaves, your wife invested heavily in Anthea Fitzgerald's business, didn't she?"

He flushed a deep maroon, then nodded, looking solemn.

"And yet you chose not to tell us that when we interviewed you."

Nigel shrugged helplessly. "I didn't think it was relevant, and it's humiliating to think not only that my wife was taken advantage of by such an unscrupulous person but that I didn't see it and stop it."

"But you did stop it, didn't you, Mr. Hargreaves? Sometime in the night, you not only took all of your own sleeping pills but those of Mrs. Cooper here, and you ground them into the tea that everyone knew Anthea Fitzgerald took before she went to sleep. And then you went into her room and drove a knitting needle into her back while she was deeply asleep and probably near death. You'd felt that she stabbed you and your wife in the back by stealing your life savings, and you wanted to punish her in the most visceral way."

Nigel Hargreaves shook his head, his eyes wide. "But I didn't. I admit I was furious with Anthea Fitzgerald, and I did come here knowing she'd be here. I thought perhaps I could talk to her and come to an arrangement." He shrugged help-lessly. "Appeal to her common decency." In a hard tone, he continued, "But she had none."

If I'd been his lawyer, I'd have told Nigel Hargreaves to clam up. Everything he said made him appear more guilty.

"And you were so furious at what Anthea Fitzgerald had done to you and your wife that you killed her."

"I tell you I didn't." His voice rose.

Then DI Barnsley said, "You'll make it easier on everyone, including yourself, if you simply admit to what you did that night."

"I won't admit to a crime I didn't commit."

Maggie Cooper spoke up then. "I'm sorry, Nigel. But I saw you and Anthea arguing, you see. The day she died. I didn't think much of it. She could be very argumentative. But later I began to wonder, and I may have mentioned I'm a trained researcher. I passed on my findings, and my suspicions, to the police."

"Our investigators were already fully aware of everything Mrs. Cooper came up with and of course were able to dig much deeper into your wife's financial affairs and those of Ms. Fitzgerald."

DI Barnsley began to rise, staring at Nigel Hargreaves, who looked stunned by this turn of events. "You'll need to come to the station, sir."

"Are you arresting me?" Nigel cried out. "For murder?"

"I'm asking you to come to the station, sir. That's all, for now."

"But you plan to arrest me." He glanced around the table in panic. "I shall need a solicitor. I—I don't know what to do."

I was looking around the table, feeling the churn of

emotions, and caught Lucy's eye. Both of us were feeling that something wasn't right.

And yet, as the detective pointed out, Nigel Hargreaves had known Anthea Fitzgerald would be here, and he'd signed up for the retreat deliberately, hoping to get back the money she'd as good as stolen from his vulnerable wife. I could well imagine his fury when she stubbornly refused to give back the money.

But still, I didn't think Nigel Hargreaves had killed her.

But if he hadn't, then who had? Who had as strong a motive?

I looked around. Everybody was staring at Nigel with various expressions of shock and interest and pity on their faces. It was hard to explain, but suddenly the pattern became clear to me, all the threads falling into place.

Nigel hadn't been the only one with a motive. I suddenly saw, the way I sometimes needed to step back from a design I was working on to see the complete pattern.

I turned to Rosalind Wallace. "Rosalind, are you really going to let Nigel take the blame?"

There was a moment of stunned silence, but I continued to gaze steadily at Rosalind Wallace. Her eyes widened, and that sweet, grandmotherly face softened into the kindest of smiles. "No, I don't suppose I am."

There was an awful moment when everyone went still and, instead of staring at Nigel, turned to stare at Rosalind. To say that every person in that dining room was stunned would be an understatement.

DI Barnsley glared at his sergeant, who was scribbling furiously in her notebook.

Rosalind looked at me. "How did you know?"

"I remember that you said you'd do anything for your children and grandchildren, that you'd die for them and that you'd kill for them." I had a pretty good idea what had happened, but I thought Rosalind deserved to tell it in her own words. "Why don't you tell us exactly what happened."

Her kind eyes filled with tears. "It was all my fault, you see. I was only trying to do good and be helpful. But when little Rosie started getting those terrible rashes, I looked for a cream that might soothe her. My neighbor, who keeps a completely environmentally clean home, told me about Anthea Fitzgerald's supposedly environmentally friendly, all-natural creams, and I thought that might be just the thing. I bought loads of the stuff."

She put a hand over her eyes, her voice choking. "I blame myself. We kept rubbing that cream into Rosie's skin...

"Then the same neighbor came to me a few weeks ago. She'd found a thread online where people were saying the cream was bad. She'd thrown hers out and suggested I do the same. I couldn't sleep. Couldn't rest. I found a laboratory and paid to have the cream tested." She had to stop and take a breath, which came out more like a sobbing gasp.

"It was full of chemicals that have been banned in this country because they are carcinogens. That means they cause cancer."

Maggie leaned over and rubbed her back. "I'm so sorry, Rosalind."

"That evil, evil woman. How could she sell products she knew were deadly? All the while masquerading as a saintly person who wouldn't even eat an egg as she didn't want to upset the hen?"

"It's not your fault," Maggie said soothingly. "You couldn't have known."

"That cream I'd been buying, thinking I was doing Rosie good, was actually making her more and more ill. That horrible, evil woman, she gave my darling granddaughter cancer. She didn't deserve to live. I'm proud to have killed her. Proud to have removed her from the face of this earth so she cannot hurt anybody else."

Maggie patted her shoulder. "I'm so sorry, Rosalind. I can't imagine what it's been like for you."

Nigel looked quite stunned. "So, let me be absolutely clear, Rosalind. You killed Anthea Fitzgerald?"

She nodded. "I did." As though relieved to be confessing, she continued, "And I must apologize to you and Maggie for taking your sleeping tablets." She seemed to gather herself. "I don't think I planned to kill her, but when I was searching her website and social media, trying to determine where she was really sourcing her creams from, I discovered she was coming here." She turned to me. "It's no reflection on you, dear. I'd planned to come anyway. Perhaps there was a moment when I wondered if I should cancel this retreat, but no, I determined to face the woman who'd made my Rosie so ill. But then I met her and saw the way she was pushing that poison to all of us. Shameless, she was. Absolutely shameless. When I asked her, quite pointedly, if all her ingredients were natural and locally sourced, she insisted they were. Evil, lying charlatan!"

She shuddered and took a sip of water. "I also travel with sleeping pills. Fortunately, I had a full bottle with me. But I worried I didn't have enough to do the job properly, so I'm afraid I took your tablets, Nigel and Maggie, added them to the ones I'd brought and bashed them all to powder, then put the ground tablets into the tea that woman kept in her room. About two in the morning, I went into her room to make certain she was dead and saw that tube of cream on the bedside table. I was filled with such rage, I'm afraid I lost my head a little. Her knitting was sitting there in its bag, and I took one of the needles. Well..."

"Oh, my dear," Maggie said, patting her friend's shoulder awkwardly.

"I see," Nigel said, looking shaken. "That's cleared that up." He turned to DI Barnsley. "Then may I assume I'm not going to be arrested?"

Poor DI Barnsley looked like this whole thing had gone in a completely different direction than he'd imagined. He said, "For the moment, yes."

I suspected he was just trying to save face. Obviously, he had a confession, and Rosalind had had the strongest motive of all to kill. Love. To protect an innocent, or that was how she saw it, anyway.

DI Barnsley pulled himself together and said, "Mrs. Wallace, we'll need you to come to the station with us."

"Yes, of course. I understand." She turned to Nigel. "Jennifer was right. I wouldn't have let them arrest you. I'm so very sorry she hurt you as well."

Maggie looked quite upset. I wondered if she'd miss her rival now at all those knitting retreats. She said, "But Rosalind, you'll have to go to jail. Whatever will you do there?"

Her beautiful face lit up in that sweet, grandmotherly smile. She said, "I shall knit."

CHAPTER 21

*O*nce the police had left with Rosalind Wallace, I think we all felt drained. The stress of the past few days was over.

Maggie said to Nigel, "I'm very sorry, Nigel. It was me, you see, who gave the police all that information about you. I'm an excellent researcher, you see, and I felt there was more that you weren't telling us."

"I do understand, Maggie. And that's an excellent skill set you have, by the way. I didn't think it was relevant to tell the police about poor Joan's declining mental health and how she had been so easily manipulated by that awful woman. But now I see that it just made me look guilty."

Agatha spoke up. "Rosalind must have meant that horrible fortune cookie for Anthea. You must have received it by mistake, Beatrice."

"Yes, I suppose so," Beatrice agreed.

"She must have intended it for Anthea, but with all the dishes being passed and the tea being drunk, the cookies got mixed up."

I saw Lucy shudder. "I don't suppose Anthea receiving the warning would have changed the outcome."

"No," Maggie said, sounding sad. "Rosalind was very clearly determined to do away with the woman she believed harmed her granddaughter."

"Was it true, though? Could that cream have given Rosie cancer?" Elliot asked her.

Maggie shrugged. "I'm not a doctor. I think what matters in this case is what Rosalind believed. Once discovering there were carcinogens in the cream, she became convinced that Anthea had caused her beloved granddaughter to develop cancer. I'd hazard a guess myself that the original rash was part of the child's illness. But, as I say, I'm not a doctor."

"Well," Lily said, "I suppose there's no need for us to stay here any longer." She glanced at me. "I'm very sorry, Jennifer, but I think I'll head back to Birmingham. This hasn't been a very relaxing knitting retreat."

I couldn't have agreed with her more. "I'm so sorry, too."

Lucy and I glanced at each other, and I knew she understood my unspoken message. She said, "Naturally, we'll refund you all your money."

Lily was the first one to say, "No. It wasn't your fault that your knitting retreat turned into a murder scene. Besides, I've nearly finished my scallop shell sweater, being forced to sit there and knit with nothing else to do. In fact, if you have another retreat, I would love to come."

I was stunned that they were being so generous.

Sunita nodded her agreement. "I think this is a beautiful place to have a retreat. I would also like to come again."

Nigel Hargreaves looked at Maggie. "What about you, Maggie? Would you come again? Now that your friend won't be here to spur you on to greater achievements?" There was a kind of twinkle in his eye, as he'd obviously seen as well as I had that the rivalry between Maggie and Rosalind probably made them both better knitters.

She said, "I'll come if you come. If you can forgive me for giving the police information that suggested you might be a murderer."

He laughed softly. "I suppose that was my own silly fault, being so filled with pride that I wouldn't give them information that I suppose did make me look somewhat sinister. But because I hadn't killed the woman, it never occurred to me that anyone would suspect me."

"I'm very sorry I did." She shook her head. "And the one person I never expected it to be was Rosalind." And then she turned to me. "How did you work that out, Jennifer?"

How had I? "I don't know. I was sitting listening to you all, and when Nigel proclaimed his innocence, it sounded so sincere. I was thinking about how if he'd killed Anthea, it was out of love for his wife, but then if he went to jail, who'd visit her? It didn't make sense." I couldn't tell the group that Rosalind's name was in Anthea's customer database without having to explain how I'd come by the information, something I wasn't prepared to do. Instead, I went with, "I thought, what if she bought Anthea's cream believing it was all-natural? I could absolutely see Rosalind putting that cream on her granddaughter, and when you were talking about the ingredients definitely not being local, I was surprised that Rosalind didn't make more of a fuss. It occurred to me just now that she already knew. I remembered her saying she'd die for those she loved and she'd kill for them. She killed out of love."

Lily rose and said, "Well, if you'll all excuse me, I think I'll go and pack."

Beatrice said, "It's a beautiful day outside. Before I leave, I'll take a walk. It's lovely along the coastal path, and I do feel we've been cooped up rather a long time."

Issy, who'd been pushing a bracelet around her wrist, glanced up at that. "Would you like some company?"

We were all quite surprised. It can't be said that Isabel had made a point of being friendly with anyone other than Elliot. After a startled moment, Beatrice said, "I'd be delighted. Thank you, my dear. It will be nice to have company."

Elliot glanced up and said, "I was going to ask you for a walk this afternoon, Issy."

I think we all waited for her to make her excuse to Beatrice and choose Elliot's company instead, but to my surprise at least, after a slight pause, she said, "That's okay. Maybe we can do something later."

He looked slightly put out but shrugged and said, "Okay."

Everyone left the dining room to pack. Lucy said she wanted to call Rafe and update him. I sat in the dining room, scanning the list of customers. Why did I not feel satisfied? I was positive that the police had the correct murderer, but something was still bothering me. I'd seen Rosalind's name in Anthea's customer database, but I thought I'd recognized another name. And as I perused the names in the database, I saw something that made me gasp.

Now I understood why the unease I'd felt hadn't left.

I jumped out of my seat and ran.

CHAPTER 22

J glanced at my watch. It had been half an hour since everyone had left the table. A terrible foreboding gripped my chest.

Where was Lucy?

I saw her in the garden walking up and down, her phone to her ear, no doubt telling Rafe everything that had happened. I had no time to waste. I threw on my shoes, dashed out the door, and began to run. Faster than I'd ever run in my life.

The coastal path is beautiful, especially on a sunny day, but I had no time to look at the view. I kept running. I was out of breath, but I dragged in air and pushed myself on. I couldn't bear it if there was another tragedy.

I passed a couple of dog walkers, who gazed at me as though I was an odd sight, which I no doubt was, gasping for air and sprinting along in clothes not meant for exercise.

I veered around a family, too winded to say "excuse me," and kept going. The path was windy, so I couldn't see far ahead, and the breeze and my own exertion were making my eyes water.

Would I be too late?

I kept running, trying to ignore a stitch in my side and a pain in my chest.

And then I saw them. Isabel and Beatrice locked together in a precarious position by a cliff. If either or both of them went over, it would be the end of them.

I halted, dragged in a breath.

"Stop," I yelled. "Don't do it."

I could barely get the words out, I was panting so hard. And then they turned to look at me, Isabel and Beatrice, and I realized tears were streaming down both their faces. And they weren't locked in a battle for survival but were hugging each other.

I went up to them anyway just to make sure, my heart pounding and my breath coming in short gasps.

Beatrice said, "Jennifer, whatever's wrong?"

I couldn't tell her the terrible thing I had thought. I simply said, "I wanted to make sure you two were okay. It can be dangerous in certain sections of the path."

Isabel looked at me, shocked. Her face crumpled. She staggered backwards and sat down on a rock. "You knew, didn't you?"

I shook my head. "Not until just a few minutes ago."

She looked miserable. "I wouldn't have done it in the end. Not really."

I sat beside her. My legs were trembling, and I was still struggling to get my breath back. "It was you who sent Beatrice the warning in the fortune cookie, wasn't it?"

She stared at the ground and nodded. "I knew we were

having dinner at a Chinese restaurant and even phoned to make sure they had fortune cookies. They're all made in the same factory, so it was easy to go to a Chinese restaurant in London and gather up a few. I wrote the message on my computer, printed it off and replaced the message in one of the cookies. Then when I was leaning over, pretending to get more food, I replaced your original fortune with the one I'd made." She heaved a sigh. "I'm sorry."

Beatrice went and sat beside her and took her hand. "It's been a very difficult time for all of us, and I think my husband and your father wasn't quite honest with either of us."

Issy had begun to sob now. "I thought it was my fault when he left. My mother said he'd been lured away."

Beatrice shook her head. "That wasn't true, Issy. I promise you it wasn't true. Your father was already living on his own when I met him."

"That's not what my mother said. She always said you stole him from us and wouldn't let him have anything to do with any of us."

Again Beatrice shook her head. "Isabel, I'd have loved to welcome Gerald's children into my life. It's not that he didn't love you, but I think knowing he'd left you all made him feel uncomfortable and reminded him that he hadn't been a very good father, so he became a worse one, an absent one. I believe he thought sending money was enough."

"He always sent a birthday and a Christmas card with a check, and I know he paid for my education. But I wanted my daddy."

Beatrice rubbed her back. "Of course you did."

"And then, when he died, I thought you'd killed him."

"No. He was a difficult man, your father, but I loved him. It was true what I said, he started out with a cold and then it seemed to turn into the flu. I begged him to see a doctor, but he was very stubborn. He wouldn't. By the time I realized how ill he was, it was too late. I called an ambulance, but he was gone when they arrived. If I'd been stronger, forced him to see a doctor, called the ambulance sooner, perhaps they could have saved him."

Isabel said, "Mother said you were a black widow, that all your husbands had died. And then when Daddy died, she was convinced you'd murdered him."

Beatrice wiped a tear from the corner of her eye. "I never murdered any of my husbands. I think I've been particularly unlucky." Then she looked at Isabel with something like hope. "But perhaps now we both know the truth, we might have lunch one day."

Isabel sniffed and wiped her streaming eyes. "I'd like that."

Now that my heart rate was back to normal and I didn't have to worry so much about Isabel pushing Beatrice off a cliff, I felt so drained of energy it was hard for me to walk back. But the three of us turned our steps back together.

Isabel said, "How did you find out that Beatrice had married my father?"

"It wasn't until this morning when I came across a list of Anthea's customers. There was a Huntington-Cole on it, but it wasn't Beatrice, it was Isabel. That's when I realized you must be Beatrice's stepdaughter, one she'd never seen."

She looked startled. "I bought something from Anthea?"

"You must have. You were in her database."

She shook her head. "I don't even remember. It must have

been something I bought online and didn't like enough to bother buying again." Then she made a funny sound. "What a strange world it is. We all came to this retreat thinking we didn't know each other, and yet somehow we were all connected to Anthea."

I looked at her. "But you did know that Beatrice was coming, didn't you?"

She nodded and addressed herself to Beatrice. "I've kept an eye on your social media for some time, and when you announced that you were coming to this retreat, I thought, why not? I wanted to meet the woman who'd broken up my family and killed my father. I may have had some crazy idea of pushing you to your death, but I couldn't have done it."

Beatrice reached over and pulled her into a one-armed hug. "Of course you couldn't have. You're not a killer." Then she said, "I would never try to replace your mother, but it would be nice if we could be friends. You're the closest thing I'll ever have to having my husband back. You're very like him, you know."

Then it was the turn of both me and Isabel to stare at Beatrice. "You knew who I was?" Issy said, stunned. "All the time?"

"Not immediately, no. I knew he had a daughter named Isabel, and something about your mannerisms reminded me of him. Perhaps he had once mentioned that your mother's maiden name was Sterling—I'm not positive—but yes, by the end of the retreat, I was fairly certain you were Gerald's daughter."

"But when you agreed to go for a walk with me today, did you know I was thinking about pushing you over a cliff?"

She laughed softly. "You might have thought about it, my

dear, but you were never going to do that. And it was a chance I was willing to take. What I really wanted to do was get to know you better."

"I'd like that too." Then Isabel laughed. "But perhaps not over knitting."

~

Thanks for reading *Scallops and Sorcerers*. I hope you'll consider leaving a review, it really helps.

While you're waiting for Jennifer's next adventure, read on for chapter one of *The Vampire Book Club*:

~

THE VAMPIRE BOOK CLUB, CHAPTER ONE

HAVE you ever wondered what your life would be like if you'd made one crucial decision differently? What if you hadn't married that man that everyone said was perfect? If you'd taken the job you wanted instead of that one with the good medical benefits? What if you'd moved to New York after college instead of Seattle?

I used to imagine what would have happened if I'd taken the other path. Maybe not the road less traveled, just not traveled by me. It was a harmless exercise to pass the time while I toiled at my boring job, safe from any threat of change.

Until one day I messed with fate.

And I was punished.

I got change all right. More than I could have imagined.

My staid life was uprooted. My road was forked. Frankly, I was forked.

At forty-five, I was both divorced and widowed (from the same man), I lost the secure but dull job I'd had for ten years, and the powers that be sent me across the sea to Ireland.

It all happened so fast, my head was still spinning when my Aer Lingus flight from Seattle landed in Dublin. From there, I took a train to Cork. It was early May, and as I looked out the window, I began to realize why they called Ireland the Emerald Isle. It was so vibrantly green, and between fields of cows and sheep, ruined castles and cottages, we stopped at pretty-sounding towns and cities to let passengers on and off. I smiled when we passed through Limerick and started making up rhymes in my head. They weren't very good, but they passed the time.

There once was a misguided witch
Who tried a man's fate to switch
Her punishment set
To Ireland she must get
But better than feathers and pitch!

From Cork city, I got a bus, though I vowed to come back and explore the pretty city when I was settled. Finally, jet-lagged and travel-weary, I arrived in my new home. The town of Ballydehag.

The bus let me off in front of Finnegan's Grocery. As the curly-haired driver retrieved my two heavy suitcases from the storage compartment underneath the bus, I thanked him. He replied, "Good luck to you, ma'am."

There's a way of wishing a person luck that sounds like

you actually wish them good things, and then there's a way of wishing a person good luck that sounds more like, "What on earth have you done?"

I was wondering what on earth I'd done, too, but I was here, now. I pulled my phone out with the address of my new home and then stared vaguely about me. I had no idea where I was, except that this was clearly the main street of a pretty Irish village. The street was lined with shops. A couple of old men in caps sat outside a coffee shop regarding me. I wondered if the arrival of the bus from Cork was a big event. And didn't that say a lot about how exciting this town was?

I couldn't think of anything else to do but go into Finnegan's and hope whoever worked there might know Rose Cottage.

I didn't think my suitcases would even fit through the narrow front door of the shop, and besides, this didn't look like much of a high-crime area, so I pushed my two cases up against the white plaster wall and walked in.

It was like stepping into the past. Narrow rows with shelves of groceries stretched from ceiling to floor and seemed to contain everything from eggs to pest-control products.

I heard voices and turned to the right and the only check-out. A plump woman with curly gray hair stood behind the counter. She wore a green cardigan with the sleeves rolled up past her wrists and all the mother-of-pearl buttons done up. The edge of the sweater was scalloped, and the collar of a crisp, white blouse framed her face. She was gossiping with two customers who stood on the opposite side of the counter. "Hello?" I interrupted.

The three stopped talking and all turned to stare at me. I

smiled brightly and tried to look nonthreatening. "I'm wondering if you can help me. Do you have the number of a taxi?"

They all looked at each other as though they had never heard the word taxi before. "A taxicab?" I tried again. "I'm trying to get to a place called Rose Cottage. Do you know where that is?"

The man, tall and thin with pale blue eyes, looked as though a great puzzle had been solved. "Rose Cottage. Ah." He nodded. The other two nodded as well.

There was silence. Me again? "Could you direct me to Rose Cottage? I have two suitcases outside. I was hoping to get a cab to take me there."

The man scratched his head. "I could fetch me wheelbarrow."

The woman behind the counter shook her head at him. "A wheelbarrow. Honestly. I can drive you around, love. It's not far. Danny, you come and stand behind this counter, and if anyone wants to buy anything, you just write down what it is, or they can wait until I get back. I won't be a minute."

Was this woman actually going to leave her post to drive a complete stranger? "I don't want to take you away from your work," I stammered.

"Oh, it's no trouble. And you've chosen a good time. We're not very busy."

Danny looked quite pleased to walk behind the counter and stand there very importantly. He began tidying up open packs of chocolate bars as though he owned the place.

"I'm Kathleen McGinnis," said the woman who'd come from behind the cash desk. I warmed to her immediately, but

I'd warm to anyone who was willing to drive me to my new home. "And you must be Quinn Callahan."

I did a double take. "You knew I was coming?"

"I've been on the lookout for you." Her Irish accent was still a novelty to me, and I could have listened to her the way I'd listen to a bedtime story. And the way I was going, with jet lag and all that had gone before, I'd be asleep before we reached Rose Cottage.

We came out of the shop onto the sidewalk, and Kathleen McGinnis took one of my heavy suitcases while I took the other. We rattled and rolled the cases up and around the corner to where a small white van was parked with Finnegan's on the side of it. She opened the double doors at the back of the van, and we hefted my suitcases inside. I nearly bumped into her as we both walked to the driver's side door, then realizing my mistake, I walked around the front of the van and got in beside her. I wasn't used to this driving on the left-hand side of the road thing and cringed as she pulled out onto the main road, not that I needed to worry. There was zero traffic.

When they had told me I was moving to a village, I don't know what I'd expected, but I'd imagined a bit more life than this. We drove down the main road and turned right and then left, and I could see the sea spreading out in front of me. In less than five minutes, she was pulling up in front of a cottage that made me cry out with pleasure. If someone had said to me, "Picture a storybook Irish cottage," Rose Cottage was exactly what I would've come up with. To start with, it was well named. The walls were white plaster, but there were climbing roses all over the front of the cottage beginning to bud. "The cottage is named for the roses, of course, and they are a sight. In a month or two, there'll be red and white and pink roses, an absolute picture. And the scent of them is heaven."

There were stone tubs in front of the front door, empty now, but I could already see them blooming with whatever I could find around here to plant in them. It was surrounded by lawn of that wonderful green color that they only seem to have in Ireland, and there was a wishing well out front. For the first time since I'd left the States, I felt there was a possibility I might one day be happy again. "This is so beautiful."

"I'm glad you like it. We hope you'll be happy here." I hadn't missed the word We. I suspected that Kathleen McGinnis was more than a shopkeeper. "I'll just show you around, let you know how things work, and then I'll have to get back to my shop."

I completely understood she'd be abandoning me very soon. That was fine. What I really needed was a nap. The way I felt now, I wouldn't wake up for days.

We pulled my cases out of the back and dragged them up the prettiest winding stone path to the front door. It was oak and solid, and the doorknocker was a Celtic knot. She took out a set of keys, disappointingly modern, and opened the front door. She stood back so that I could go in ahead of her. I wished silently that it would be as pretty inside as it was out and then dragged my case across the threshold. I walked into a square entrance way with hexagonal red tiles on the floor, hooks for hanging coats and a pine chest. From there, I walked into a beautiful, comfortable-looking front room. Two blue sofas with cushions and woolen throws flanked an old stone fireplace already set with the wood for a fire. The carved wooden mantel was lined with candlesticks each holding a fresh golden beeswax candle. Bookcases were crammed with titles I couldn't wait to get my hands on. However, the best feature of the room was the windows looking out on the craggy coastline and the ocean. I went to the window and looked out. This part of the coastline was nearly deserted but for a castle standing proud but very lonely on a promontory set back from the water. I could imagine that back in the day, it had been an excellent spot to watch out for enemies. But now it just looked lonely. The gray stone was relieved by green ivy covering the inland side of it.

"Kitchen's through here," said Kathleen, dragging me away from my reverie. I followed her voice across the hall and into a kitchen that wasn't large but was clearly the center of this house. The floor was flagstone, and the wooden cupboards had been painted a cheerful shade of blue. Inside a nook that had once been a huge fireplace was a stove that filled me with dread. "What is that?"

"Have you never seen an Aga?"

"No. Is it electric?"

She laughed at me. "It takes some getting used to, but you'll grow to love it." She explained how one stoked it for the day. The stove would keep my cottage warm. I wasn't too keen about this stoking business. Was I going to be chopping wood? I wondered if I'd have to walk to the village pump and get my day's water. Not for the first time, I wondered what I had done. But then, what choice had I had?

There was a small fridge that looked familiar and modern enough that I thought I could manage it. A farmhouse sink sat under a pretty window. No sign of a dishwasher. Kathleen opened the fridge, beckoning inside. "I stocked it with a few basics. There's milk and bread and cheese and eggs and so on." And then she moved to one of the cupboards and opened that. "And here's tea and coffee and some biscuits. Just a few things to get you started, my dear. In the fridge, you'll also find a pot of my own mulligatawny soup, in case you don't feel like coming out this evening. You may just like to get settled. Of course, if you want some company or something else to eat, there's always the pub, O'Brien's. Or The Painted Beagle—that's a bistro that serves food all day. Otherwise, there's just a coffee shop."

On the scrubbed pine kitchen table was a ceramic jug, filled with wilted flowers. She *tsked* with annoyance. "I knew I forgot something. I meant to freshen the flowers." She mumbled something that sounded like *"floridium ad vivum"* and waved her hand over the vase, and the flowers jumped to attention and perfect freshness. "That's better."

"So you are a witch. I wondered."

She chuckled. "I am at that, and I'll help you get settled and such."

She came and put her hand on my shoulder. It was a comforting gesture. "Why don't I make you a cup of tea, my dear? You look dead on your feet. Go and sit in the lounge, and I'll bring it through."

I knew I should let her get back to her shop, but the truth was, I didn't want to be alone right now. I said tea would be nice and, instead of going into the living room, I watched her. I thought I'd better get a handle on how to do things here. It didn't look that complicated to make tea. She took a perfectly normal electric kettle and plugged it in. From one of the cupboards, she fetched a blue ceramic teapot and two mismatched china mugs. Whoever had lived here before me had obviously loved flowers. They were covered in flowers, one in roses and one in what looked like pansies and daffodils. Kathleen opened a packet of shortbread biscuits and settled them on a blue china plate and, by opening several cupboards, even found a tray. I didn't talk much, just watched her efficient movements, and then when she was done we took the whole thing through to the living room. I settled into the surprisingly comfy couch, and she sat beside me and placed the tray on a slightly beaten-up but charming wooden table.

She poured the tea. I couldn't stop looking out the window at that beautiful view.

I didn't know how to start, so finally, I said, "Was this hers? The woman I'm replacing?"

Kathleen's eyes were green and knowing. She smiled slightly. "You feel it, don't you? Yes. Lucinda made this cottage her home. She still owns it and the bookshop where you'll be working. It's exactly as she left it, fully stocked, and she's left instructions for how to order new books and, well, everything you need to know."

I was walking straight out of my life and into another woman's. Strange didn't begin to describe how that felt. I'd never even met this Lucinda. "I wish I could talk to her."

Kathleen shook her head *no*. It was the answer I'd expected, but it made me uncomfortable. "I don't see what harm it can do. I only want to find out more about her business and how to run it. It's a terrible responsibility to run someone else's store, and I don't want to screw up." Totally reasonable.

"Speaking to Lucinda is forbidden, as I believe you've been informed."

"Can you even tell me where she's gone?"

"Somewhere in England. That's all I know."

"Is that what you do then? Play musical chairs with witches who haven't followed the rules?"

Her soft eyes grew suddenly hard. "What you did was a terrible crime, Quinn. And you know it. We witches may not interfere against death."

ORDER YOUR COPY TODAY! *The Vampire Book Club* is Book 1 in the Vampire Book Club series.

A Note from Nancy

Dear Reader,

Thank you for reading *Scallops and Sorcerers*. I am so grateful for all the enthusiasm this series has received.

I hope you'll consider leaving a review and please tell your friends who like cozy mysteries.

Review on Amazon, Goodreads or BookBub.

Your support is the wool that helps me knit up these yarns.

If you haven't already, don't forget to join my newsletter for a free prequel, *Tangles and Treason*, the exciting tale of how the gorgeous Rafe Crosyer was turned into a vampire.

I hope to see you in my private Facebook Group. It's a lot of fun. www.facebook.com/groups/NancyWarrenKnitwits

Until next time,
Happy Reading,

Nancy

ALSO BY NANCY WARREN

The best way to keep up with new releases, plus enjoy bonus content and prizes is to join Nancy's newsletter at NancyWarrenAuthor.com or join her in her private FaceBook group Nancy Warren's Knitwits.

$\sim$

Vampire Knitting Club: Paranormal Cozy Mystery

Lucy Swift inherits an Oxford knitting shop and the late-night knitting club of vampires who live downstairs.

Tangles and Treason - A free ebook for newsletter subscribers. A paperback version is available for sale. NancyWarrenAuthor.com

The Vampire Knitting Club - Book 1

Stitches and Witches - Book 2

Crochet and Cauldrons - Book 3

Stockings and Spells - Book 4

Purls and Potions - Book 5

Fair Isle and Fortunes - Book 6

Lace and Lies - Book 7

Bobbles and Broomsticks - Book 8

Popcorn and Poltergeists - Book 9

Garters and Gargoyles - Book 10

Diamonds and Daggers - Book 11

Herringbones and Hexes - Book 12

Vampire Knitting Club: Cornwall: Paranormal Cozy Mystery

Boston-bred witch Jennifer Cunningham agrees to run a knitting and yarn shop in a fishing village in Cornwall, England—with characters from the Oxford-set *Vampire Knitting Club* series.

Village Flower Shop: Paranormal Cozy Mystery

In a picture-perfect Cotswold village, flowers, witches, and murder make quite the bouquet for flower shop owner Peony Bellefleur.

Vampire Book Club: Paranormal Women's Fiction Cozy Mystery

Seattle witch Quinn Callahan's midlife crisis is interrupted when she gets sent to Ballydehag, Ireland, to run an unusual bookshop.

Great Witches Baking Show: Paranormal Culinary Cozy Mystery

Poppy Wilkinson, an American with English roots, joins a reality show to win the crown of Britain's Best Baker—and to get inside Broomewode Hall to uncover the secrets of her past.

Abigail Dixon: 1920s Cozy Historical Mystery

In 1920s Paris everything is très chic, except murder.

Murder at the Paris Fashion House - Book 1

Death at Darrington Manor - Book 2

Toni Diamond Mysteries

Toni Diamond is a successful saleswoman for Lady Bianca Cosmetics in this series of humorous cozy mysteries.

Frosted Shadow - Book 1

Ultimate Concealer - Book 2

Midnight Shimmer - Book 3

A Diamond Choker For Christmas - A Holiday Whodunnit

Toni Diamond Mysteries Boxed Set: Books 1-4

The Almost Wives Club: Contemporary Romantic Comedy

An enchanted wedding dress is a matchmaker in this series of romantic comedies where five runaway brides find out who the best men really are.

The Almost Wives Club: Kate - Book 1

Secondhand Bride - Book 2

Bridesmaid for Hire - Book 3

The Wedding Flight - Book 4

If the Dress Fits - Book 5

The Almost Wives Club Boxed Set: Books 1-5

Take a Chance: Contemporary Romance

Meet the Chance family, a cobbled together family of eleven kids who are all grown up and finding their ways in life and love.

Chance Encounter - Prequel

Kiss a Girl in the Rain - Book 1

Iris in Bloom - Book 2

Blueprint for a Kiss - Book 3

Every Rose - Book 4

Love to Go - Book 5

The Sheriff's Sweet Surrender - Book 6

The Daisy Game - Book 7

Take a Chance Boxed Set: Prequel and Books 1-3

For a complete list of books, check out Nancy's website at
NancyWarrenAuthor.com

ABOUT THE AUTHOR

Nancy Warren is the USA Today Bestselling author of more than 100 novels. She's originally from Vancouver, Canada, though she tends to wander and has lived in England, Italy, and California at various times. While living in Oxford she dreamed up The Vampire Knitting Club. Favorite moments include being the answer to a crossword puzzle clue in Canada's National Post newspaper, being featured on the front page of the New York Times when her book *Speed Dating* launched Harlequin's NASCAR series, and being nominated three times for Romance Writers of America's RITA award. She has an MA in Creative Writing from Bath Spa University. She's an avid hiker, loves chocolate, and most of all, loves to hear from readers!

The best way to stay in touch is to sign up for Nancy's newsletter at NancyWarrenAuthor.com or www.facebook.com/groups/NancyWarrenKnitwits

To learn more about Nancy and her books
NancyWarrenAuthor.com

facebook.com/AuthorNancyWarren

x.com/nancywarren1

instagram.com/nancywarrenauthor

amazon.com/Nancy-Warren/e/B001H6NM5Q

goodreads.com/nancywarren

bookbub.com/authors/nancy-warren